Love's Coffee

Café de Maison Series (Book 1)

JANE KEENE

This is a work of fiction. Names, characters, organizations, places, events, and incidents are either products of the author's imagination or are used fictitiously.

Copyright © 2018 Jane Keene

All rights reserved.

www.janekeene.com

No part of this book may be reproduced, or stored in a retrieval system, or transmitted in any form or by any means, electronic, mechanical, photocopying, recording, or otherwise, without express written permission of the publisher.

Published by Keene Marketing

www.keenemarketing.com

ISBN: 172097568X

ISBN-13: 978-1720975687

CONTENTS

CHAPTER 1	4
CHAPTER 2	10
CHAPTER 3	15
CHAPTER 4	20
CHAPTER 5	24
CHAPTER 6	28
CHAPTER 7	33
CHAPTER 8	39
CHAPTER 9	43
CHAPTER 10	49
CHAPTER 11	54
CHAPTER 12	57
CHAPTER 13	61
CHAPTER 14	67
CHAPTER 15	72
CHAPTER 16	75

CHAPTER 17	79
CHAPTER 18	84
CHAPTER 19	88
CHAPTER 20	91
CHAPTER 21	94
CHAPTER 22	97
CHAPTER 23	99
CHAPTER 24	102
CHAPTER 25	104
CHAPTER 26	107
CHAPTER 27	110
CHAPTER 28	113
CHAPTER 29	118
CHAPTER 30	121
CHAPTER 31	124
CHAPTER 32	126
CHAPTER 33	130

CHAPTER 34   133

ABOUT THE AUTHOR   136

CHAPTER 1

"You can't be serious, Joe? How can you expect me to leave my Billy alone for the weekend? You must have rocks in your head if you think I would even consider it."

Taking him by the arm, she pushed him not so softly into the far corner of the room.

"Easy, there Maise, I just wanted to do something nice for you, you work so hard, I thought you could do with a break, that's all."

Maisey shook her head and clicked her tongue against her cheek. Joe wasn't good looking in the conventional manner of speaking, he had charm and many women would have fallen for it.

"I could do with a break, a break from here, yes," she gestured around the cafe, "but you know I can't be away from Billy for more than a day, he needs me, he has never spent one night away from me, he is doing so well, I couldn't think of what it would do to his progress."

Joe looked down at his tan crocodile leather shoes; they were so shiny he could almost see his own reflection in them.

"Billy is thirteen years old; don't you think it's time you thought about yourself and your own needs?" replied Joe with a note of impatience.

"Joe, I want you to listen close," he edged in nearer towards Maisey's comely figure, his lips trembled slightly at the thought of being so close to her ample bosom. "The only reason you want me to come away with you has nothing to do with me needing a break, but everything to do with you wanting to get laid!"

Caught unawares, Joe jumped back into the magazine rack causing newspapers and magazines to slip and slide all over the floor. Maisey stepped forward and pushed her finger into his chest,

"You don't think that I haven't noticed you practically undressing me with your eyes every time I walk past you. What did you think would happen on this so-called 'break'? Did you think that I would be so grateful to get an opportunity to leave town for a while that I would just happily fall into bed with you out of gratitude?"

By now the commotion had started attracting the attention of the other patrons, looks of interest and concern turned to their direction. Joe, red-faced and fully aware of the attention, tried to gain his composure. He pulled at the hem of his sea-green collared shirt and looked at Maisey, pure hatred spreading across his face, he grabbed Maisey's arm and picked up a strand of her honey blonde hair in his other hand, twirled it around his fingers, and whispered loudly in her ear.

"You little tart! I can't believe I wasted all this time on you! You nothing but a washed-up has-been, one day you will be begging for attention from me like a stray dog. And, you know what I do with stray dogs? I kick 'em!"

At that moment, a large hand calmly removed Joe's sweaty paw from Maisey's arm.

"I'm going to give you ten seconds to leave my premises, if you do not leave in those ten seconds I will show the rest of my customers what I do to customers who I don't believe are always right."

"Alright, alright Mick, no need to get all tetchy, just keep your workers on a lead in future," with one more withering look directed at Maisey, he skulked out of the café.

"Are you ok Maise? Take some time to sort yourself out; I will get Breda to cover the rest of your shift."

"No, it's grand. I'm fine, Mickey. I should never have let it get so far. I knew I wasn't interested, but I didn't have the heart to tell him to get lost."

Mickey could see the hurt in Maisey's eyes, she was such a wonderful woman, and she did not deserve to be treated so badly. He had never understood women in general. Even his Evie, God rest her soul, had been a puzzle to him.

He watched Maisie walk off; she planted a fake smile on her face and carried on serving the customers. Mickey leaned against the door post at the back of the coffee shop, he folded his arms and let out a slow sigh, he was proud of what he had achieved over the past ten years, the Café was doing well, and it had an excellent reputation. Its comfortable feel combined with modern touches finished with contemporary lighting and high ceilings, made it a popular choice with the young and old alike.

But it was not always so easy; the time after Evie's death was too painful to think about. He referred to those times as the "dark ages." Dark, because he could not see his way out of the pain, and unfortunately, each day he had tried to seek solace at the bottom of a scotch bottle.

Where would he have been if it had been for…?

"Mick! You're needed out back, Big Tom Rafferty has brought the fresh produce, and he refuses to deal with me, only the boss will do for Himself".

"Thanks, Ryan, you'd better get back to your beloved machines, there are some ladies queuing for their daily fix, but maybe it's not only for the coffee." Mickey nudged Ryan playfully and made his way out back.

Ryan strode purposefully towards the coffee bar; he flipped the counter lid skillfully with one strong arm while reading the coffee orders in the other. He diligently focused on the task at hand making sure no mistakes were made, he never attended any fancy barista courses, but he knew coffee and he sure knew how to make it, latte's, cappuccinos, mochas, he made them all with such proficiency.

"So, tell me, Luv, where did ya get to be so good with ya hands?" Mrs. Jenkins, the owner of the hair salon next door was not so subtle in her appreciation for Ryan. Ryan knew she had a soft spot for him, but he dared not encourage her, not with Mrs. Jenkins' "man-eating" reputation. "I have had a lot of practice, Mrs. J", answered Ryan professionally, he used the shortening of her name purposely to emphasize the difference in age between the two of them, and he certainly did not want her to get any funny ideas.

"I was just saying to our Angela, that with hands like yours, you should be working in my salon".

Ryan gave out a throaty laugh, "Me in a salon? Now, that's a gas. No, Mrs. J, I can safely say I'm where I belong."

He handed her, her coffee order, she gave him a wink with a heavily made-up eye, turned on her obscenely tall, post-box red high-heels and swaggered towards the cashier.

Ryan's attention suddenly caught by the beautiful brunette at table 10, he could not take his eyes off her, every day at the same time she would come in. Her dark chestnut coloured hair hidden in a demure bun; her piercing green eyes and porcelain skin. Cheekbones that would put any top model to shame. He shook his head and turned to his next order.

At that moment Maisey was getting ready to take her order.

"Miss, are you ready to order?"

"Mm, what? Oh, yes right. Yes, just the cappuccino for now, thanks". Victoria put her head back down and buried herself into the report she was busy with. How could she allow herself to get so distracted? She had been so focused on her work up until that moment. She heard his laugh from across the room, the sound rumbled down, fast through her body like a gumball falling through the machine after a coin had been dispensed inside of it.

She purposely sat with her back towards him, but now that her attention was disturbed, she could not help but turn around, she watched him move around the coffee bar, his pale skin set off by his short clipped black hair.

She didn't usually like men with facial hair, but there was something about the shadowy-beard neatly dispersed across his chiseled jaw bone that made her mouth dry and her brow sweaty.

She continued to watch him move, and pull levers expertly, his tattooed bicep flexing and stretching to the rhythm of the coffee machines. Victoria stuck her arm up and beckoned Maisey to her table, "Mm, excuse me, waitress? Please add an extra shot of espresso to my cappuccino."

Yes, Victoria thought, with a perfectly manicured hand, she tugged at her starched white shirt cuffs and pulled them over her expensive Cartier watch, the strong coffee should certainly bring back my focus.

CHAPTER 2

Maisey had finished her early shift at the café; she was spending the afternoon with her mother. "Mam, of course I'm getting out and about, and before you ask I haven't had a date for a few months, but I have been busy."

Not wanting to bring up her mornings un-pleasantries with Joe. Maisey felt incredibly irritated, this was the same conversation she had been having with her mother every month for the last few years.

"Maisey, dear, what is it that keeps you so busy that you don't have time for yourself? You are in your prime; you have a lovely figure and a beautiful complexion. With a little maintenance, haircut and a bit of makeup; you would look fabulous and totally irresistible."

"Oh Mam, you make me sound like some prize cow, I don't have time for that now. Have you seen the men in this town?

They are either after one thing, care more about their own appearance than you or I do, or they are over the age of fifty, no offense, Mam. My life is very full with Billy and the Cafe for starters."

Maisey looked at her mother, she was in pretty good shape for her age, her hair was perfectly cut and set. Maisey could see tiny flecks of grey in her mother's golden, corn-colour hair, but it did not make her old, but more sophisticated. Just then a commotion from Billy's room wrenched their attention, followed by intense screaming and shouting. Maisey was quite used to this, she ran towards Billy's room, which was not too far. Although her flat was neat and modern, it was incredibly small and pokey.

Maisey found Billy in a heap on the floor in the middle of the room, he was crying with frustration. Maisey calmly approached him, talking softly and soothingly, she knew if she tried to touch him now he would start shouting again, eventually after five minutes, Billy had stopped crying, he allowed Maisey to put her arms around him and help him up off the floor.

She sat him down on the bed.
"I'm sorry, Mam. I was only trying to fix my model airplane, but the glue wasn't working," Billy blubbered out the words; his shoulders shaking up and down from crying. Maisey's heart ached for her child, it had been ages since he had made such a big scene, he was making excellent progress with the new group he was enrolled in.
"Never you mind, my dear. We will get you better glue tomorrow. Why don't you go wash your hands and put on your favourite movie? I will clean this up. When dinner is over, we can sit together and fix your plane. Would you like that?"
Billy's facial expression changed, and he started to smile, he nodded his head eagerly, he got up off the bed and loped past his grandmother who had been standing in the doorway of his bedroom.
Isabelle watched her daughter cleaning up her grandson's mess on the floor, pieces of model airplane debris strewn across the room. Maisey really got dealt a tough hand in life. At one stage, everybody thought Maisey would be living the high life on Broadway, her dancing career ended abruptly with a horrific fall during a

performance, this meant her ankle would never withstand the demands of a professional dance schedule.

She never really fully recovered from the news. Then, she met Paul; she was so young and vulnerable and what could they say about Paul? He was a rotten good-for-nothing. As soon as he heard Maisey was pregnant, he up and did a runner.

That was almost fourteen years ago, and nobody had heard from him since. Maisey was left with the responsibility of bringing Billy up all by herself.

The biggest blow was finding out that Billy was on the autism spectrum. Fiercely independent, Maisey refused to take help from her parents, she wanted to raise Billy on her own, the only money she accepted from her parents was for Billy's therapy. Everything else she labored hard for in the Cafe.

Billy had come a long way and was making progress. He was doing well in school, and he even trusted Isabelle to look after him, but it was Maisey who could not let go of the reins.

Isabelle followed Maisey into the kitchen, "Dad and I were thinking, we are prepared to lend you the money for that Business Management course you are interested in".

Maisey picked up the drying cloth and sighed, "That's very kind of you, Mam, but who will look after Billy? The course is in the evening and it's twice a week, I'm not sure if I can give over so much of my time."

"Well, I have discussed it with your father and he has agreed that for the duration of the course, Billy could stay with us on Tuesday and Thursday nights. It will give you some time to work on your own without any distraction. We will set up a room, and we will let him choose all the decor that will go in the room, which should make him feel that he is at home. Come on, what do you say?"

"Mam, in theory this would be great, but you know how Billy is about change, I really don't want him to regress in his program, he has worked so hard."

"I know, Love, but don't you think it's time to do something for yourself? You are going to be 38 years old next birthday, and you have not spent any time on yourself for over thirteen years. You are still young and have so much still to do".

Maisey, shook her head, her mam did have a point. "Okay, how about we try this, before I'm due to start the course, why don't we test to see if Billy would be comfortable at yours? I don't want to commit myself to something and Billy hits a wobbly, and I have to give up half way. What do you think?"

"I think that's grand, my girl, I really do, and I think we should start this next week".

Maisey looked at her mother, and suddenly laughter just bubbled up, and she couldn't stop laughing. At first, Isabelle thought her daughter had gone mad, but soon she too was laughing. Billy came running through, "what's wrong, Mam, Nan?" He asked with concern. Maisey cupped his beautiful angelic face in her hand, "Nothing's wrong, my darling, in fact hopefully all will soon be fine." They both did not quite know what was so humorous, but the laughter felt good, she almost lighter afterwards.

CHAPTER 3

It was a Monday morning and things were hotting up in Victoria's office. "Liz, would you get that darn phone, it has been ringing nonstop all morning! Where the hell are you Liz...?"

Victoria hated inefficiency, her usually super organized PA was MIA, and all hell was breaking lose.

"Oh Vicky, I'm soo sorry," Liz came puffing out of breath into the room, "Orla from Accounts caught me on the stairs, she was in a state about her sister leaving for New York".

"Liz, you are super lucky that you are so good at your job, and that you are my best friend, and what have I told you about calling me Vicky at work, it makes me sound like a little girl skipping in the school yard. You know I have a reputation to protect. Please get onto these calls, and push tomorrow's appointments back for an hour later, I have a meeting with the big boss, fingers crossed it's about the partnership". Victoria clapped her hands excitedly, a gesture rarely seen, but clearly this meant a great deal to her.

Liz sincerely hoped for her friend's sake that the meeting would bring Victoria's big dreams to fruition.

Liz sat down at her desk and started working in Victoria's diary; she was the only person who knew about Victoria's past. It was completely opposite to Liz's upbringing with ponies and overseas holidays. As far as anyone else was concerned, Victoria looked as if she was from a privileged background, private school educated. How far this was from the truth! Vicky grew up in a small village outside

Limerick, she was an only child and her parents had tried farming, but with no success. Her dad had a problem with the drink, he was never violent, but it meant that whatever money they had was used to support his habit.

Her mother attempted to make up for her dad's shortcomings, but it was no use. From a young age, Victoria learned to count on one person in her life and that was herself.

She was educated at the local parish school; she was incredibly smart and earned herself a place in a top college in Dublin.

Liz had met Victoria when they worked together in the college bookshop. At first, Liz thought Victoria was a snobbish cow who had airs about herself, but she quickly learnt that Victoria was incredibly driven, and was not going to let anyone stop her from reaching her goals.

She remembered the first time they had gone out together to a local pub, Victoria looked so uncomfortable and out of place. Victoria so regal, held herself upright, which gave the appearance of her looking down on people.

Liz sniggered to herself as she recalled the icy reception Declan Flannery received from Victoria as he tried to chat her up. Word got around the college that Victoria was a hard target, so she was not bothered by many suitors; only the very brave or very thick skinned attempted and failed miserably.

Anybody who saw Liz and Victoria together would think that Victoria would definitely be the one to have a boyfriend, and not the other way around. Liz was by no means unattractive; she was cutesier and pretty as in the girl-next-door kind of way. They made such an odd friendship, one tall, one short from different backgrounds, but somehow it worked, and they clicked.

Liz's thoughts were disturbed by the buzz of her phone, she picked up the receiver quickly, "Liz! What is the matter with you today? I have been calling for over two minutes! Have you finished the changes in my diary? Also, Mr. McCarthy from Steelworx is on his way, he phoned me directly. Evidently, there is some emergency with the merger, and he needs advice pronto! Could you ask Mari to organize tea?" Victoria was very much aware of not making Liz do her dogs' body work, Liz was her assistant, and she was determined to use her in the work she was doing, not to go fetch and carry coffee, dry cleaning or lunch.

About ten minutes after, Liz accompanied a very flustered looking Mr. McCarthy into Victoria's office.

By the look on his face, Victoria started to feel very nervous. "Bruce! How nice of you to come over personally, I was quite intrigued by our phone conversation earlier." Victoria extended out her hand, and personally led him to a comfortable black leather chair in front of her antique oak desk.

Mr. McCarthy sat down and brushed both hands down his face in a sign of distress. "Victoria, unfortunately this is not a social visit, I have come to warn you", he cut off suddenly, looked around to the door uncomfortably, and then at Liz. "Bruce, whatever you have to say to me, you can say in front of Liz, I trust her with my life. You are making me very uneasy with your behavior".

He began again in half a whisper, "Victoria, what is your relationship like with your colleague, Dermott Freeman?"

Victoria stared at him and answered abruptly, "What the hell does that have to with anything, I demand to know what is going on, Bruce? This sounds all very cloak-and-dagger, and I don't like it!"

"Dermott is setting you up, Victoria, and he is using the Steelworx merger to do it!" He suddenly blurted out.

Everyone in the room was quiet, Victoria stood up slowly, and Liz reached for the chair next to Mr. McCarthy.

"What, what do you mean, setting me up?"

"Well, he has made some back-end deals with Colcor, and what it means is that he is setting you up to take the fall when the merger fails. I can't prove it, but a good source informed me of a rumour going around. Victoria, I know you. And, I know you would never lie or cheat for your own gain. That's why I'm convinced it's Dermott! He is the only other person who has worked on this and been in the meetings. Does he have anything to gain by dragging your name in the mud?"

Victoria was shocked to the core; could this be why her boss wanted to meet with her tomorrow?

"Bruce, before I react, can you be sure your source of information can be trusted? If it's a just a rumour, could we not squash it and make it somehow go away?"

"Victoria, I can assure you the source comes from inside Colcor, this is serious, and somebody is seriously gunning for you, you have to react quickly".

"Why, that slimy, little scum-sucking snake!" screamed Liz jumping from her chair. "I can honestly see him doing that, he is after the partnership, Victoria. He hates you! He can't stand that you have risen through the company ranks faster than he has, I see the way he looks at you, and it's him!"

"Liz, please calm down, I can't go around accusing him without proof, and I'm not even sure what the dirty deal I am apparently involved in entails." Victoria got up from behind the desk and started pacing the room.

"Bruce would you be prepared to help me? The merger cannot be compromised. I know my career is hanging in the balance, but my first duty is to my client."

Victoria felt sick to her core, waves of nausea followed by a quiet rage, just when she thought she could relax a bit in her life, this has to happen.

If that dirty toad Dermott was backstabbing her, he had another thing coming. Nobody was going to take away everything she had worked so bloody hard for, nobody!

CHAPTER 4

"Hey, Ryan, easy on that boxing bag, what did it do te ya?" Ryan broke from his rhythm and looked up, he was absolutely soaked, completely lost in the mesmerizing dance with the punching bag he had almost forgotten where he was.

He gestured to the bag and shouted, "Hey Jimmy, aren't you glad you not the bag?"

"Ayah, be off with ya! Ya could never take on the great Jimmy McGeary!" he punched the air and jumped around demonstrating his point.

Ryan laughed loudly, it sure felt good to just relax and enjoy his surroundings. He had been coming to Jimmy McGeary's boxing club since his early teens. It was the only place he truly felt accepted, nobody was interested in where he came from or what he did on the weekends. The fellas from the club had one thing in common, and that was boxing, that's what they focused on and that's all they spoke about.

Ryan admired Jimmy. He was a former middle division champion, someone who peaked a too soon in his career. Instead of falling to pieces over his failures, he started the boxing club to help nurture young fighters' passion for the sport.

Ryan grabbed his towel and water bottle, and headed to the showers, it was still early, but he wanted to get to the cafe' before the others.

He had a few calls had given him his own set of keys years ago, which caused great upset to the other cafe workers.

His life had not always been this complicated. He had an extremely ordinary upbringing; in fact, his parents still lived in their family home in Swords. He had two younger brothers, they all were married, and each of them had three of their own children.

Ryan knew his parents were worried about his life of solitude. It wasn't natural for a man his age to be on his own. Ryan looked in the mirror, with all that had happened to him, he sometimes expected an old man to stare back at him from the glass.

He had many regrets, he knew he caused many of his parent's grey hairs; he was such a troubled teen.

School had bored him to tears; Father Joseph had always said he was too clever for his own good. He was exceptionally bright, but misguided. A rebel by nature, he went against the grain, got himself into a lot of trouble especially when he became involved with an inner-city gang. At first, the antics they got up to were harmless, just destructive boy stuff, graffiti, turning over bins. But things got serious when the gang crossed paths with Jack Mulligan, who ran a drug ring, an incredibly dangerous thug who did not hesitate to take matters into his own hands when he felt it was necessary. Jack did not have enemies because he made sure that anybody who got in his way was well and truly dealt with.

Most of the guys stuck around to join Jack, the promise of money and an easy life was too tempting, but Ryan had never gone into the drug pushing side of the gang. When he realized what was happening he made the decision to turn his life around and leave the gang, but the only problem was he knew too much about the gang's internal workings; Jack had made the lads suspicious about Ryan's move.

Things came to a head when Jack threatened Ryan's family. Ryan made the biggest decision in his life and he went to the Gardaí and reported his own gang. And, that's how Ryan helped bring down one of the largest drug kingpins in Ireland.

Jack was sent away for fifteen years and a large part of his gang was sent to serve time. After this tumultuous time, Ryan was only nineteen and decided he needed to study and focus on his future. He found his passion and talent, IT.

At the age of twenty-four, Ryan sold his company for a small fortune, and be independently wealthy, he works at the café to be anonymous. Even though Jack was in jail, he still had an eerie feeling that he had not seen the last of him.

Ryan arrived at the cafe', he unlocked the doors and walked in. He loved being there early on a summer's morning, the sun filtered neatly through the blinds. It was the complete sound of silence that comforted him, he knew the potential for noise and chaos, and he just stood in the middle of the room and took five deep breaths.

It was time for the dreaded monthly phone call, but he knew he had to do it; his solicitor had eyes and ears on the streets for any sign of a threat to his family.

Ryan had been blessed with good health, but he kind of felt that waiting to hear the news of an illness progressing and waiting to hear that your family is potentially in danger might be close to the same feeling. That sick dread in his stomach each time he made the call.

He made his way to Mickey's office and sat down behind the extremely neat desk. My goodness, Mickey was particular. Ryan wondered what Mickey's reaction would be if he switched things around on the desk?

He dialed the oh-too-familiar number and drew in a ragged breath. "Seamus, my man, talk to me. Set my mind at ease." Ryan did not believe in pleasantries; his heart sank as he listened to Seamus.

"What do you mean I have to watch my back? Jack still has five years left on his sentence!" After a few moments on the phone to Seamus, Ryan shakily hung up the phone, and then in a fit of rage threw the phone across the room, causing all Mickey's neatly piled papers to scatter onto the floor.

CHAPTER 5

"My goodness! The Café sure is busy this morn, I feel positively run off my feet." Maisey mopped her brow with some kitchen towel, she stretched her hands over head. She preferred to be busy during the day, but this was ridiculous.

Most of the customers were new faces, it seemed like the new customers had scared the regulars away.

Breda was in a mood and didn't care who heard her, "I swear if I have one more request for a refill coffee, there will be murder. Damn Mickey and his breakfast special! All these folk are from the conference centre down the road, typical office workers, they see a freebie and take advantage of it".

"Calm down now, Breda, it's not all bad, the breakfast special is just running for two more days. And, to be honest the tips have been good, the less they think they are spending on food, the more they have left to give to us" reasoned Maisey brightly.

"Ah, I suppose you are right. I better get out of the kitchen and earn some tips. I have a hot date on Friday night with the new guy who works at the gym, and that means I need the works done at the salon." Breda licked the top of her index finger and tapped it on her hip making a hissing sound as she marched back onto the restaurant floor.

Maisey watched Breda smile and flirt with her customers, she honestly was the limit.

Breda was tall with an athletic frame, long dark hair that swished as she walked. Although Breda was extremely attractive, her beauty was tainted with a worldly hardness.

Maisey often felt a bit envious of Breda, she was young and free to do anything that she pleased.

Breda tapped her fist on the counter top, "Ryan, do you have you those two Americanos; I need them for table three?" "Hello Ryan! Are you there?" taunted Breda; she really was quite annoying when she wanted to be. Ryan handed over the coffees and glared at her. "Aren't you sparky today?" Breda spun around and delivered the coffees to the table. She passed Maisey on her way to the kitchen.

"What do you think is up with Mr. Handsome? He nearly threw the coffee at me a moment ago. He might be gorgeous, but I know there is something off with him. I tell you he is dangerous, you will never catch me alone in a dark alley with him."

Maisey laughed aloud, "That's because you are just sore that he has not made a move on you." Breda pulled a face at Maisey and stalked off toward the kitchen.

Maisey felt a bit protective over Ryan, it wasn't because she fancied him, he was a few years younger than her, and it was more a sister-brother relationship anyway.

She walked over to the coffee bar and leaned over. "I would watch Breda today, she thinks you are dangerous."

"Well, maybe Breda is not that wrong," said Ryan sharply. He turned around and carried on with the coffees.

Maisey felt a bit taken back, what the hell is going on with everyone today? It's not like her life was easy peasy breezy now, but she never let on that she spent most days barely keeping it together, planting a smile on her face all day long until late at night when Billy was sleeping, and she was all alone, she would often sit and cry quietly to herself, and let the tears stream down her face.

It was not easy being a single mom to a child with special needs, but it was her business and she refused to take it out on other people.

Billy had been particularly difficult this morning, which nearly caused her to miss her bus. The essay she had to write for her Business School application was not going well; she had been up all night working on it.

Maisey had been a fair student at school, but she felt so old, rusty, and stupid. Besides, when you were destined to be a world-famous dancer. Who needed to remember the rules of grammar for that? Maybe Mickey could help her? After all, he does own and run a business.

In the afternoon, Maisey made her way swiftly to Mickey's office, although the crowds had thinned there were still some patrons left in the cafe.

She knocked on the door, and went in. "Mickey, do you have a moment?"

"Anything for you, Maise. How can I be of assistance?" he pushed his chair away from behind the desk and clapped his hands together.

"I need you to look at my application essay for business school. I'm not sure I'm coming across as interesting, or intelligent enough. I need an unbiased opinion. I can't ask me Mam, because I know she will "ooh" and "ah" about it just because I'm her child."

Mickey nodded his head and answered; "I can't guarantee I will be able to contribute a great deal, but I can certainly give it a try."

Mickey reached over the desk to take Maisey's essay. "Thank you, Mick. I certainly hope it does not bore you." She came around to the other side of the desk and leaned over to give Mickey a peck on the cheek.

Maisey left the office, but she quickly turned to look back at Mickey, was he blushing? Maisey suddenly felt a little uncomfortable, she didn't mean anything by giving Mickey a quick kiss on the cheek, and she had done it countless times before, why would it be any different now?

CHAPTER 6

The next morning found Victoria poring over documents. She had been up all night without stopping.

"Victoria, take a break. You have been going over those documents for ages." Liz walked around Victoria's desk and put a comforting hand on her shoulder.

"You right, Liz, I'm going around in circles here, everything looks above board, but I know if I look close enough I will get my breakthrough, and finally have the evidence against Dermott. My head is throbbing".

"Why don't you take a break, go for a walk, and grab some coffee at the place you never take me to."

Victoria laughed, "How do you know about the Café?"

Liz laughed and answered, "That my dear friend is a secret, but as your best friend and assistant, I do take it upon myself to know everything about you." Liz bowed dramatically and flounced out of the office. Victoria picked up her coat and purse and headed for the door.

Yes, this was a good idea. She would take a walk and go to the only place in the world where she felt she could think and recharge her batteries for a few moments. The sun was trying ever so hard to peak through the tough exterior of a massive wall of clouds, but the sun too was having a tough time. It was late in May, but winter did not seem like it wanted to let go.

As Victoria walked down the road, she observed the people on the street, the vans delivering fresh produce to the trendy delis, the mothers pushing babies and toddlers in prams, people shopping.

She pushed the heavy glass doors of the Cafe open, she had to wait a few moments for an elderly couple to leave, but it gave her a chance to take in the sight that was her sanctuary, the aroma of the coffee and pastries, the sounds of conversations that she will never be a part of. Even though she had only ever been here by herself, she didn't feel sad or lonely. She was thankful that her usual table was open, and she headed straight for it without waiting to be seated.

"Oh my, look who just waltzed in," Breda whispered not too softly to Maisey.

"Yay for me. I guess I better put her order in before she starts snapping her fingers at me," grumbled Maisey back to Breda.

Maisey went over to the coffee bar, "Ryan, Miss High-and-Mighty's usual please". "I'm on it already, Maise, I saw her when she came in."

"Wow, you are observant today," retorted Maisey.

"I don't see why you and Breda have to give her such a hard time, it's not like you actually know her. Or is it that you two are just jealous?"

Startled by Ryan's outburst, Maisey hastily grabbed the order and headed toward Victoria, who seemed to be a little out of sorts. She was digging around in her purse looking very flustered.

"Here's your coffee, will you be having your usual?" Maisey set the cup awkwardly down in front of Victoria. "Thank you, but I think today I might try one of your cinnamon buns and do you have today's papers? I need my daily news fix."

Well, clearly this was a day for surprises. First, Ryan overreacting about the fussy customer, and now Miss High-and-mighty changes her usual order, and speaks an actual sentence to her.

Maisey shrugged slightly and went to fetch a newspaper for Victoria.

"Blast, I can't believe I forgot my laptop!" Victoria felt very spare, this was the first time she had been here without her laptop, or some work to do, she did not know what to do with her hands or where to look.

She took out her phone, but there was only so much she could do, and she soon gave up on trying to read old messages.

She was trying ever so hard not to look in Ryan's direction, but she couldn't help it. He was wearing a black short sleeve V-neck t-shirt, it was fitted, but not too tight. Victoria could see he worked out at a gym or did some kind of physical activity. Ryan suddenly turned around and looked directly at her, she got such a start she dropped a sweetener sachet into her coffee.

She felt her face redden, she took the spoon and proceeded to fish around her cup to remove the offensive white mass of sweetener out of her cup of coffee.

Before she could finish, another fresh cup was placed delicately in front of her. It was not the usual waitress, but Ryan. She had never been in such close proximity to him. Her hands were clammy, and she had to force herself to look up at him. His eyes were a dark cobalt blue, her mouth was so dry again, and all she could squeak out was a croaky, "Thanks."

Ryan, usually full of confidence, stood there for a moment, nodded his head in affirmation, turned and walked back to the coffee bar.

Mickey, who had been watching this exchange, he tapped Ryan on the shoulder, "Not very smooth, why don't you go back and talk to her?"

"What are you on about, I just got her another coffee, no biggie".

"Ryan, you never leave your station to serve customers personally. I thought Breda was going to have a heart attack when she saw you standing there."

"That's not saying much if Breda makes a fuss, she makes a noise about everything. Besides, if there was any truth in what you are saying, you know I couldn't do anything about it, so what's the point of starting something?"

"You can't cut yourself from the world, you have to live. It's natural for young people to go out and meet other people".

"Mick, I made my choice years ago, when I went against Jack. I knew I wouldn't have a normal life. How could I bring a new person into the circus of my life? It would be too complicated and too risky. Besides", he gestured towards Victoria," this one's only for looking at". He stood and drank in the sight of Victoria, even if he could date her, she was not his usual type; she was too polished and poised. He gave a sigh, turned around and resumed his duties.

On the other side of the Cafe, Victoria felt as if she had run a full marathon, her heart was still pounding against her chest, she managed a few sips of the mocha, but her mouth still seemed dry. The cinnamon bun she ordered was sitting on the plate mocking her. What on earth made her order it?

Suddenly, everything felt wrong, she needed to get back to the office.

She gestured for Maisey, "Could you please get my bill ready?" Maisey picked up the plate with the untouched cinnamon bun, "Do want this to go then?"

Victoria looked at the cinnamon bun and pulled a face. "No thank you, maybe I should stick to smoked salmon on toasted rye next time". She handed Maisey a twenty-euro note and made her way out of the cafe, making a conscious effort not to turn around and look at Ryan.

CHAPTER 7

When Victoria got back into the office, there was an urgent message on her desk from her boss, Mr. Stevenson. She had mixed feelings about the meeting, especially since hearing about Dermott's possible betrayal.

Estelle ushered her quickly into his office. She tried to gauge by the look on Mr. Stevenson's face if this was going to be friendly or a fight.

"Aaah! Victoria, good of you to come so quickly." "Like I had a choice," she said to herself. "Please take a seat." Mr. Stevenson stood up and gestured for her to sit. It was very difficult to tell how the meeting was going to go, he was being very polite. He started into it straight away.

"Victoria, you are the most suitable out of all the candidates for partnership, you are most certainly the most efficient and thorough solicitor we have ever had at the firm. You are one tough cookie."

This took her by surprise, "Thank you Sir, you know me I am just doing my job the only way I know how."

Mr. Stevenson smiled weakly; Victoria knew something negative was going to happen. "We are just concerned; we have been hearing rumblings, certain rumours about your possible involvement with the Colcor scandal."

Victoria felt her stomach sink to the floor, "Mr. Stevenson, I can assure you those rumours are just that, they are rumours, they are unfounded and completely untrue. I have only ever conducted myself with honesty and integrity. There is obviously somebody out there who is looking to ruin my reputation. I intend to find them and bring them to justice." Victoria stressed her point by beating her fist onto the boardroom table, causing poor timid Estelle, Mr. Stevenson's personal assistant, to jump and drop her pen. Victoria sat back in her chair and tried to gain her composure again.

Mr. Stevenson leaned forward, the sun catching the side of his steely, grey head, his hair, cut and combed to perfection. He raised a commanding hand, indicating to Estelle that she need stop taking minutes.

"Victoria, can I offer you some advice, off the record? You need to make sure when you find the person who is ruining your name, that they must be punished. I personally feel sorry for this person, whoever they may be, will have to face your wrath. But in doing this, we need to keep the name of Lewis & Stevenson out of any scandal, we support you one hundred percent, but we also need to protect our interests. I hope you understand this, our clients value our professionalism."

"I understand completely. Anything I do professionally will be above board, I can assure you." Victoria stood up and shook Mr. Stevenson's outstretched hand. And, anything I do personally, well, I don't have to tell you, Victoria thought to herself.

She walked out of the boardroom, she had a splitting headache, she didn't feel like going home to an empty house. So, she routed round in her cream Louis Vuitton bag for her phone, she wanted to call Liz to see if she wanted to go out for a drink.

"Where is my stupid phone?", she lamented to herself. She remembered she had not used her phone all afternoon; she had been in a meeting this afternoon and had not even checked her messages. She tried to recall the last time she used her phone. The memory was like a smack in the head. Of course! She left it at the Cafe'! In her rush to leave, she had thrown her things into her bag, thrown money at the waitress and left.

I need my phone, I have to go back to the Cafe, I don't want to go back there, but I have to. Pull yourself together girl! Hopefully he won't be there, it's almost closing time. Surely, he can't be there all the time? She tried to reason with herself. She made her way out of the building.

All the while she was walking down the road, she kept reciting a silent mantra to herself, "I can do this, you are a kickass law machine, and you can do this!"

She reached the Café only to read the "Closed" sign hanging on the door. "Oh crap!" She exclaimed and did a half jump in frustration. What am I going to do without my phone; I will have to come here first thing tomorrow morning.

She was making all sorts of plans in her head when she heard the door unlock behind her. Expecting to see the owner, an older man, she turned around and planted a bright smile on her face, only to be surprised by Ryan standing before her.

Her smile slipped off her face, and she became all self-conscious and awkward again. He smiled at her, an intense heat rose up from her legs right through into her belly, like warm arms of longing engulfing her body. It almost felt like the time she had taken her first sip of whiskey.

He seemed to be waiting for her to do something, "Oh, you are wondering why I'm hanging around outside your door, well not your door personally, but the Cafe door, you see I left my phone here at lunch and I've come here to collect it."

"Sure, come in," Ryan answered, "I will go and check Mickey's office. All personal items left behind are stashed there." He gestured for her to sit at a table and wait for him. She had never heard him speak out aloud before, and for some reason hearing his voice unnerved her even more. She had hoped his voice would be high and squeaky like a neutered chipmunk, then she would be put off him, but it was the complete opposite. His voice wreaked havoc on her senses, she kept imagining what her name would sound like coming from his lips. Mm…those lips, she wondered what other delights would be possible from those lips.

"Ahem, here is your phone," Ryan gestured toward Victoria, who was caught unawares and lost in her thoughts.

"Oh, aah, thank you." Victoria reached over and took the phone from him, but as she took the phone, searing heat raced through her fingers as they accidentally grazed Ryan's hand.

They both looked down at their hands and pulled away suddenly. Victoria painfully aware of Ryan's close proximity, stood up too quickly, causing the chair to fall over and the contents of the table to scatter.

Victoria took a step back, but trod on the fallen chair, which caused her to tumble backwards. Just as she was about to fall, she felt a pair of strong arms envelop her and Ryan pulled her towards him.

This must be what heaven feels like, wondered Victoria. She had a strong urge to run her hands down his muscled back, and cup his ever-so firm buttocks. She had been a long-time admirer of his rear, and had likened it to a green, crisp and juicy apple. The muscled mounds she knew would be hard, but silky to the touch. Oh, my goodness, what am I thinking? Victoria untangled herself from Ryan's arms picked up her bag and almost ran to the door.

She sub-consciously knew the door was locked but she continued to rattle it in hope that it would miraculously open.

Ryan strode over to the door and unlocked it, but before he let Victoria out, he moved close to her and looked deep into her eyes.

"By the way my name is Ryan, what is yours?" Victoria looked at him from under her eyelashes and quietly answered in a barely audible whisper.

"I'm Victoria."

"Victoria" Ryan repeated her name almost as if granting her earlier wish. And yes, as she knew it would, her name off his lips left her feeling quite giddy. She stepped out into the cool evening air and walked shakily towards the car park.

Ryan closed the door and rested his head against it for a few moments; he had never experienced such intensity before. He had to use every bit of restraint not to tilt Victoria's head back, so he could kiss the delicate pulse on her creamy white neck. His level of arousal was off the charts. He could not go home feeling like this, he needed to expend some energy. Maybe he would go back to the gym. All he knew was that his first instinct was right, he had to stay away from Victoria; it was too dangerous. Next time, he might not succeed in holding back; he had to make sure there wasn't a next time.

CHAPTER 8

"Buzz!" The sound of doorbell reverberated around the small second floor flat. "I wonder who that could be at this time of the night, Billy." Maisey asked as she got up cautiously to answer the door.

"Oh, good evening Mick!" Maisey crossed her arms over her chest, suddenly very aware that she was not wearing a bra under her well-worn former navy blue, but now grey sweatshirt.

"Sorry to disturb so late in the evening, but I have finished going through your application essay and I wanted to give it back to you."

He started to hand over a large Manila envelope.

Maisey waved her hand and said, "I'm sorry, where's my manners, do you want to come in for a moment?" She gestured towards the kitchen. She didn't want Billy to get excitable so late at night, it was best if he didn't see Mick. She walked over to the kettle, "Would you like a cup of coffee?" "No, no, I'm not staying long I just wanted give you your essay back."

"Thanks, Mick, but it really wasn't necessary for you to come out so late at night, I'm working tomorrow you could have given it to me then".

"Well, I was out this way and just thought the quicker you get it back the sooner you can submit your application." said Mickey awkwardly.

"Oh right, umm, so what did you think?" Asked Maisey cautiously.

"Of what?" Replied Mick all confused.

"Of my essay, what did you think of it?

"Oh, yes, it was good, really good, I could not see anything there that needs any changing. It's perfect".

Instead of feeling flattered by his praise, Maisey felt slightly uncomfortable. It was the way Mickey was looking at her. Mickey looked up and realised Maisey had caught him in mid stare. His face flushed a bright red, he clapped his hands together and said, "I had better get going now, see you tomorrow at work." Maisey nodded and walked with Mickey to the door. She waved him off and closed the door behind him.

"Was that Uncle Mickey?" Billy came running towards the entrance with the newly rebuilt model aeroplane.

"No, my love, it was friends of your Nan's. Now run along go and brush your teeth." Billy looked slightly disappointed, but Maisey did not feel too bad for telling a little lie about Mickey's visit. Billy was very fond of her boss, but he would have been too over-excited by the visit. It would have taken her forever to get him to settle down and go to bed. And, Maisey needed to get some sleep tonight. She had a full shift tomorrow and needed time to make final edits to her application essay.

Later that night, as soon as she rested her head on her pillow, she could not shake the feeling that somehow something was different between her and Mickey. Could it be possible that Mickey had feelings for her? Surely not, he was twenty years older than her. But how could she explain, his sudden awkwardness around her? It was all very disturbing. This did not help her quest to go to sleep. When she awoke the next morning, she felt as if a city bus had run over her, and to make matters worse she had woken up in a sweat with the image of Billy running around after Mickey shouting, "Daddy!"

***

"Ryan, I don't think that's a very good idea, you have been in trouble with the law before." "I don't see what other option I have, Sean." Ryan looked down at the gun that lay on the kitchen table. Ryan could see the panic in his brother's eyes.

"I know this looks extreme, but after what Seamus told me, there might be a possible hit out on me. I have to be prepared. I want you to take the whole family including Mom and Dad out of the city and go to the bungalow. The "bungalow" in question was a six-bedroom beach side manor in county Donegal.

It's the summer holidays you should have time off. I just need to know that everyone is safe."

"Have you even gone to the authorities with this information? You can't expect us all to disrupt our lives so that you can run around playing cops and robbers!"

Ryan saw red. He grabbed Sean by both shoulders. Both men had a similar build, but Sean knew that if they ever got into a scuffle, Ryan had the ability to afflict more damage.

"I know you were quite young when all this went down last time, but they nearly killed our folks, they will stop at nothing to hurt the people I love, you need to take this seriously! Feck! This is about people I love being in danger! How dare you think I would in any way enjoy being on some vigilante crusade? Jack runs with a dangerous crowd and will stop at nothing to get his revenge."

His grip on his brother's shoulders had tightened and suddenly he dropped his hands. He picked his coffee cup off the marble counter top and walked to the kitchen window. On a normal day he had good view of the bay. But he stared out for a few moments, not really looking at anything in particular.

"Ryan, I'm sorry if you think I'm making light of this situation. If it is really as dangerous as you say, I trust you and I will take our family away, but please promise me that you will watch yourself. Mam would be devastated should anything happen to you." Sean walked over and patted Ryan's shoulder.

"I can watch myself, but I could never forgive myself if anything happened to anyone else. I brought this to the family, it's only right that I sort it out!" vowed Ryan with steely determination.

Sean walked to the front door, and said, "I had better get back, Moira would skin me if I'm in late. She will think I used you as an excuse to have a pint at the pub." Ryan shook hands with his brother and closed the door behind him.

CHAPTER 9

Victoria awoke the next morning feeling confident and positive, she was sure she could sort the mess her career was currently in. She decided to skip the gym and eat a leisurely breakfast at home. She set the little bistro table in her modern kitchen, rye toast with egg and a berry smoothie. She sat down, took a sip of her coffee and opened the paper. She scanned the features and flicked through the society page. Something drew attention back to an article on page two. Victoria read the byline "Top city solicitor implicated in fraudulent deal." In the distance, Victoria heard glass breaking, she looked down to see her coffee cup in pieces, scattered shards lying on top of the sparkling white Italian tiles, brown liquid everywhere.

Her phone was ringing; she answered it on the third ring. "Liz, this can't be true, have you seen the Daily Times article?"

"Vicky, that's exactly why I'm phoning, I can't believe that cretin had the audacity to leak the story. I'm in the office now, and I wanted to warn you that this is all everyone can talk about."

"Aargh! This is bad, really bad! I'm ruined I will never be able to work in this country again! What am I going to do? The Gardaí are going to get involved. If I cannot prove my innocence, I could be disbarred or even worse go to jail!"

Victoria could not stop pacing up and down, she had forgotten about the glass on the floor. "Can I call you back, Liz I have another call on the line".

"Wait Victoria, please don't sound so defeatist, we will catch Dermott in the act and get the proof we need, please do not give up." Victoria said a quick goodbye, took a deep breath and answered the next call.

"Hello Mr. Stevenson, I was just about to call you".

"Victoria!" barked Mr. Stevenson "We have a big problem, that news article has the potential to do massive damage to the practice. It doesn't take rocket science to guess which "firm" was being referred to in the article. We have to distance ourselves from the sensation; I'm afraid Victoria, we are going to have to ask you to take a leave of absence until this all blows over, paid of course."

Victoria felt her stomach sink, she felt so nauseous, and she could hardly speak, eventually after a moments silence on the line, Victoria replied, "Mr. Stevenson, I really do not think that this is the best way to deal with the issue, this is what whoever is trying to frame me wants. I could do so much more if I was in the office." Victoria realised her voice had a pleading edge to it, but she was desperate, she was desperate to hold onto her job. Her life consisted of going to work, what would she do with herself all day? Like bile in the back of her throat, panic rose up.

"What about Liz? What will happen to her while I'm away?"

"We have made arrangements with Liz to work with Dermott. With you out of the office, he will have to pick up your case load."

"What!" screeched Victoria, forgetting that she was on the phone. "You can't do that Des!" Victoria had forgotten formalities and reverted to calling Mr. Stevenson by his first name. "Dermott is the reason I am in this mess, now you are rewarding him by giving him my clients, and my personal assistant. Will you be giving him my office too?"

Victoria was enraged. "Now hang on Victoria, you cannot go making random and wild accusations against fellow co-workers. Do you have proof that Dermott is trying to frame you?" Asked Mr. Stevenson.

"Well not exactly, but I have received information from a good source warning me against Dermott."

"So, no actual hard evidence against him?"

"No, but that's what I was planning to prove".

"I'm sorry this is happening to you, Victoria, but without decent evidence against Dermott, your allegations could land you in more trouble. I suggest you stay out of the limelight, consult your own legal counsel and hopefully this will all blow over soon."

Victoria let out a sigh, she felt completely deflated and defeated. "It's easy for you to say Mr. Stevenson, you are not the one who stands accused of Industrial Espionage." "Could I at least come into the office today and fetch a few files? I promise not to hang around too long, and dirty up the office halls." With a sulky goodbye Victoria hung up the call, she slammed her head into her hands.

After about fifteen minutes of staring into space, Victoria picked herself up from the table. She would not let Dermott win! She would go down to the office, fetch what she needed, hold her head up high. She had not done anything wrong.

She was the injured party here. She decided to shower and dress. Since she did not have to go into work, she decided she would dress casually, but super saucy casual. One thing her mother had taught her was that even if you did not feel good, dressing up and making an effort can help you feel better about yourself. No business suite today, she got out a pair of blue Tommy Hilfiger skinny denim jeans, a small white camisole, and heeled black ankle boots. She would leave her long chocolate brown hair down for once. Not too much makeup and she was ready. She grabbed her purse and her black biker jacket from the coat stand and left the house.

It did not take her long to get to the office; it was mid-morning, so the traffic had calmed down.

She felt extremely conspicuous as walked passed the reception desk. It seemed as if everybody knew.

"Oh, my goodness, you look amazing!" Liz came running up to her en route to her office. "Liz, I am so glad to see you!" said Victoria, she gripped Liz and gave her a hug, an extremely rare show of emotion.

"Can you believe that Mr. Stevenson has me working for Satan himself? I was so mad I almost quit, but then I remembered I have a mortgage to pay off and my holiday in Corfu is coming up." Liz looked down at her hands guiltily, "I'm sorry I'm such a coward."

Victoria hugged her friend again, "Liz, you are not a coward. I would never expect you to leave your job for me. Don't worry about me, maybe this is not as bad as we think." Victoria unlocked her office door, and ushered Liz in quickly. She closed the door and began pacing up and down the room.

"You, working closely with Dermott might work to my advantage; you could see what he has been up to".

"Vicky, you are right! I hate that ejit, he makes my skin crawl". Liz shuddered.

Victoria was about to reply there was a knock at the door, but before Victoria could answer the door opened.

"Aah! Victoria. So surprised that you are in today, aren't you on "holiday"?"

Victoria felt sick, she could not believe Dermott had the audacity to come and gloat in her office. He reminded her of a weasel. His hair was mud colour brown, which for some reason he thought looked good by fully gelling it back. He moved closer to Victoria and put a pale pudgy hand on her back, which she promptly swatted and moved behind her desk. "

I must say, Vick, you really brush up well, not that you look bad in your power suites, but you should wear your hair down more often, it gives you a softer look." Dermott's eyes wondered down the length of Victoria's body. Revulsion for this disgusting human washed over Victoria, but she knew she had to control herself, and that he was purposely baiting her. She replied with all the patience she could muster.

"What do you want Dermott? Even though you believe I'm holiday, I still have a lot to do, and this little exchange is wasting my time."

"There's no need for you to be so formal and law-like with me, we are old friends." He moved back closer to Victoria, he got up so close and whispered close in ear, she could feel his vile coffee-tainted breath on her neck.

"Because when all this is over that's what you going to need, is friends".

Victoria could not control herself anymore. She turned around and slapped him through the face. Liz let out a gasp of surprise. Dermott put a hand to his face and walked to the door, "You will regret that move, my dear!" With a slam of the door, he left the room. Victoria slunk back down into her chair, the whole episode had frazzled her, she had fought tough lawsuits and won, but this was so personal to her, she felt so vulnerable.

"Liz what am I going to do?" was all she could ask.

CHAPTER 10

Later that afternoon back at the Café, Mickey and Ryan were sitting in Mickey's office having a heart-to-heart.

"I'm glad you told me. Do you think they will make a move during the day, in full view of everyone?"

Mickey and Ryan were having their usual evening whiskey together. The last customer had left, and the rest of the staff had finished cleaning and prepping for the next day. It was Ryan's favorite time of day; he enjoyed his chats with Mickey. They had been through so much together; Mickey was one of the few people who really understood his situation. Ryan slugged on his whiskey and answered.

"That would be stupid. No, I think if they try, there wouldn't be many witnesses. But don't worry, I'm not taking any chances, I have hired a private security company. They have men placed discreetly outside the shop, and do a security sweep every morning".

"Do they stay with you, when you go home?" Mickey asked anxiously.

"Don't worry about me, Mick. You know I can take care of myself".

Mickey got up from his chair and put on his coat. "As long as you know what you are doing. I need to get back upstairs, Padraig is coming over to play cards, he is a grumpy ol git, I better not keep him waiting. Are you fine to lock up?"

Ryan laughed, "You ask me that every night, I have been locking up every night for over five years".

Mickey put his hand on Ryan's shoulder and said. "But this time I mean it, will you be safe to lock up on your own?"

Ryan patted Mickey's hand. "I will be grand. You go on then, you don't want to keep Padraig waiting".

Ryan started going through the cafe, checking windows, and turning the blinds. He finished quickly, grabbed his keys and jacket. As he was locking the door to leave he looked up, and across the road, he saw Victoria. Or at least it looked like Victoria. She looked so different, but good different, he was mesmerized. Her beautiful hair was cascading down her back, her clothes fitted around her shapely and slim figure. He felt a stirring in his trousers, he knew he couldn't control his body's natural reaction to her; he was only human.

His head was telling him to walk on, but he had to have one more look. He noticed that all didn't seem well, it looked like she was upset. His instinct kicked in and he crossed the road in a few strides, she was sitting at a table on the side pavement, as he got near he heard her crying. This was too much for him to handle, he put his hand out and turned her to face him. She looked quite startled but seemed to be at ease when she realised it was him. Her eyes were red from crying.

Ryan spoke first, "What are doing here? Did someone hurt you?" Victoria looked up at him and started to sob uncontrollably. He reached for her and pulled her into an embrace.

After what seemed liked ages, he led her across to the cafe and unlocked the door. His body still felt like it was on fire from where Victoria's body had touched his. He knew she was upset, but he couldn't help but feel the need to pull her close again and feel her feminine curves against him. He knew if she gave him any encouragement he would not be able to stop the physical reaction, he was too far gone now. He had felt her in his arms, it would be difficult to erase those feelings. He tried to bring himself back to earth. "Victoria would you like a coffee?" She looked up at him and nodded sedately.

***

Victoria had been so rattled by her encounter with Dermott that she took to the streets and just started walking. She had been walking for a few hours and she honestly did not know how she had landed up at the pub across from the café, she had ordered a drink and sat outside. She had tried to hold it together, but she was overcome with fear over her future. She was so shocked when Ryan came across her, even more by her reaction to his embrace. Every nerve ending in her body was on high alert; she couldn't deny it anymore she wanted it to happen again. After months of stolen glances and illicit daydreams. It wasn't just an appreciation for something good looking, it was a whole lot more. She wanted him to touch her, judging by how good it felt when he hugged her she now felt compelled to find out more.
She watched him making coffee, his hands looked so masterful, pulling levers pushing buttons. The thought of his hands expertly running over her body was intoxicating. She needed to get a grip on her feelings; she had every right to blame it on her rotten day. She felt like she needed to explain herself.

"I'm sorry if I ruined your evening plans, I'm not normally like this, it's just been a very difficult day." He walked over to the table, placed the coffee cup in front of her.

He took her hand and gently pulled her up out of the chair, he shook his head and said softly, "There is no need to explain yourself."

She was about to protest when he placed his finger on her generous lips in a gesture for her to keep quiet. Victoria's base instincts took over, his fingers caused a searing heat to spread through her body she needed to feel more of him, she needed to taste him. She opened her mouth and proceeded to flick her tongue lightly on his fingertip, her tongue as delicate as butterfly wings around it seductively.

This was all too much for Ryan, he pulled Victoria close and claimed her lips with his own. Their tongues meshed in union, their bodies fitted together perfectly, crushed together by their passion. Victoria could feel Ryan's excitement, which only made her want him more. Ryan moved his hands into Victoria's hair, tugging on it slightly. Victoria, ran her hands down Ryan's back feeling the contours of his strong muscles, she cupped his buttocks and somehow knew they would be firm to the touch. In their urgent desire they had landed up against the wall in the far corner of the room. Victoria's jacket lay on the floor, Ryan now was lifting her white camisole, revealing her white lacy bra, she felt so alive, so wanton, she never wanted this feeling to end.

He was kissing the skin around her breasts; her hands were in his hair. As he kisses went lower, his lips now below her naval, she thought she would spontaneously combust. His mouth, teeth and lips continued to tease her senses.

Was it possible that she was hearing bells, the jangling sound became louder until both Ryan and Victoria realised that it was not their imagination, the noise got louder, like someone trying to open a lock. Victoria quickly threw her camisole back on, Ryan gestured for her to be quiet and pointed for her to move to the back of the restaurant. Ryan moved stealthily and reached behind the coffee station. As Victoria peaked from behind the wall, she caught a glimmer of something shiny in Ryan's grip, it took a full twenty seconds for Victoria to realise that the shiny object in Ryan's hands was a gun.

CHAPTER 11

On the other side of town, Maisey was saying goodnight to Billy on the phone.

"Good night my darling be good for your Nan and Pa. Yes, I'm so happy you are enjoying your new room, sleep tight and love you too". Maisey ended the call, she felt so relieved. Billy had been so cooperative when she dropped him off at her parents' house earlier that evening. She was expecting a huge scene, but he obediently went off and waved at her from his "new" room window.

She was now feeling a bit spare, she was not used to being on her own, the flat suddenly felt like a five-bedroom mansion. She had managed to finish her essay, she completed the supporting application papers, sealed the envelope and put it on the table near the entrance for posting in the morning.

Thinking about the application, going through approval and scrutiny made her feel nervous and anxious. Maisey tried to relax, she took her book and lay down on the sofa, but she couldn't concentrate. Her thoughts were driving her crazy, she should be enjoying the time to herself, but she could not settle down. Maisey grabbed her phone maybe she should phone a friend? She didn't have too many of those, she had been so busy with Billy she never had time to make friends other than the ones from the Cafe.

A sudden buzzing noise from the doorbell shook her from the depressing thoughts of having no friends.

Maisey dragged herself off the sofa and went to open the door.

"Omg, Maise, what the hell do you call that outfit you have on?" Maisey just stared as Breda came storming into the flat, all hair and newly spray-tanned, carrying two bottles of prosecco in her hands.

"Breda, what the devil are you doing here?" Maisey felt very confused and irritated at this sudden intrusion.

Breda busied herself in the kitchen looking for glasses, "what you mean, what am I doing here, I'm here to rescue you from yourself that's all".

"Now I'm really confused" sputtered Maisey as a glass of sparkling alcohol was thrust into her hands.

"I overheard you telling Mick that Billy was sleeping at his grandparents tonight, so I figured you would not take the opportunity to go out and have some real fun, so I thought I would bring the fun to you. Slainte!" Toasted Breda and she slammed her glass against Maisey's.

Maisey shrugged her shoulders in a sign of defeat and took a big glug of her drink, the bubbles surprisingly pleasant popping slowly down her throat.

"You do know the reason why Billy is away, it is not for me to go running around the pubs to all hours, I had to finish some important paper work and I needed some time without interruption".

"Well, are you finished then?" enquired Breda cheekily.

"Yes, I'm finished, but how do you know that I hadn't planned something else, or I could have had a bloke over for the evening?"

Breda burst out laughing, "I'm sorry Maise, but I have worked with you for over five years, and not once have you "had" a bloke over for the evening, it's not in your character. It's like you closed shop downstairs after Billy was born, if you excuse me saying ".

Maisey was quite taken back by Breda's accurate observation,

"Excuse me "Miss Drop-my-pants-for-a-kiss"! I would have you know just because I don't tell people about my sex life doesn't mean I don't have one!" With that Maisey downed her drink and walked back to the kitchen counter and poured herself another one. Breda wasn't far off from the truth, but she was not going to admit that. She had a few very brief affairs in the past thirteen years, but nothing felt right.

Maisey filled Breda's glass and asked, "In any case, why did you come here tonight, you usually have such an active social life why have you chosen me to waste one of your precious nights?"

"To be honest, I just had my spray tan done. I did not want to sit at home by myself all evening, and I thought that I couldn't show up at my regular friends' houses looking all orange and smelling like shite and that. I knew you wouldn't mind, so here I am." admitted Breda honestly.

And, there it was. Breda was about as tactful as a brick in the face, but Maisey figured at least she wasn't alone, and Breda's stories were if anything very entertaining.

CHAPTER 12

Victoria's heart was in her in throat. How the hell did she get mixed up in this mess? She was crouched on the floor in the dark at the back of a coffee shop at 9:15 at night. If the situation was not so serious, it would actually be quite funny.

Ryan was gesturing for her to come over to him at the coffee station. She tried to move as stealthily as possible, but she was a tall woman, all legs and arms hooking on chairs and tables. Honestly, she wasn't built for this cloak and dagger stuff. Eventually, she managed to crawl over to Ryan, who she now noticed held the gun firmly in his left hand. Victoria felt sick as she watched him creep slowly towards the door, all of a sudden, the Cafe lit up and the sound of a scuffle came from the entrance.

"What, the feck do you think you are doing?" yelled Mickey, he was trying to get out of the chokehold Ryan had around him.

"Goodness, Mick! I thought you were the man sent by Jack!" Ryan let go of Mickey and clipped the safety on the gun.

Victoria stood up, "Would someone please like to tell me what the hell is going on here?" Both men turned to look at Victoria, who by now had managed to get out from behind the coffee station. Although her hair was still disheveled, she had managed to straighten her clothes out. She exuded a commanding presence. This was work, Victoria not the pliable nymph from earlier in the evening.

"Oh, crap!" The expletives were just rolling off Ryan's tongue. "I'm so sorry Victoria, the last thing I wanted was for you to get mixed up in this. Everything is crazy!" He strode over to her and tried to take her hand.

Victoria subtly moved away from Ryan's reach and made her way to the table where she had thrown her handbag.

"This day has been ridiculously unreal, first my work, my reputation is shredded, and then I find myself in a compromising position with a man I barely know."

Ryan's face reddened as he felt Mickey smirk at him.

"Only then to think my life is in danger because there is an intruder, who turns out not be an intruder, but the owner of the establishment. I need to get out of here".

Ryan wanted to stop Victoria from leaving with all his might, but he knew it was for her own good to leave now before things got too heavy between them. He simply nodded, he moved to the door and unlocked it, Victoria waved a small goodbye to Mickey, who was watching the scene with great interest. He waved back. Victoria hesitated slightly as she walked past Ryan to go through the door, he thought she wanted to say something, but she turned away and walked out into the night.

Ryan locked the door and turned to face Mickey. He breathed out heavily and sat down at the nearest table.

"So, this is what you get up to when I let you lock up at night?" joked Mickey.

"Mick, I'm really not in the mood for jokes, I can't believe I let things go so far, I put her life at risk, even if it was only you tonight, it could have been your man!"

"Aaaaargh!" Ryan got up and smashed his fist into his hand. "This stuff with Jack has to end soon I can't live like this anymore!" Mickey didn't say anything, he just walked over to Ryan and patted him on the shoulder.

***

Victoria walked briskly down the road, she pulled her biker jacket closer to her body, she felt cold. Maybe it was the shock of the insanity that was her day. All she wanted to do was get home as quickly as she could, jump into a hot shower and curl up on her sofa and cry, or eat ice cream or both.

She was so tempted to throw herself into Ryan's arms before she left, but luckily her sanity had stopped her. Who was he? And what was he involved in? Who runs around with a gun, maybe he was a spy? Her law brain kicked in, with all the trouble she was in she couldn't take a chance and become involved with someone who obviously was into some shady business.

The fact that he looked like he was prepared for the situation. He looked so skilled and comfortable with a gun in his hands. And, who was this Jack she heard him tell that Mickey guy that he thought that it was "Jack's guy?" Too many questions were bouncing around in her brain.

Victoria rubbed her temples, thank goodness she was near the car park, she routed around in her bag for her car park card and proceeded to validate her parking. She felt a sudden chill, even though it was still light outside, she noticed that she was alone and started feeling nervous.

The car park was quite empty, but she had been here a million times before without feeling anxious. She felt a little silly, maybe it was all the commotion in her life making her feel fragile and vulnerable. She got into her car and started the engine. Phew! She felt somehow more at ease in the safety of her moving vehicle. Maybe she wanted to subconsciously to put distance between her and Ryan. She needed a clear head now. She had bigger problems of her own, she needed to get evidence against Dermott and stop him for good.

CHAPTER 13

"Yes, I'm outside her house now. Yes, she is alone, and no sign of Mulligan. I'm not sure what he is up to, but there is no security outside the house either. He is either incredibly stupid or playing some game. Do you think he is using her as bait?" The voice on the other end of the line growled on for a few seconds, he silently awaited his next instruction. "Not a bother, I will send the letter special delivery today" was his reply to the voice.

***

Maisey, got into work 5 minutes later than usual, she had a pounding headache, and her stomach had been doing loops all morning. Bleeding Breda and her prosecco, followed by the further ill-advised whiskey shots. They had ended up dancing on the sofa singing to eighties hits until after three in the morning.

Maisey had dug out an old bottle of whiskey she had in the press for when her father came around to visit. The last time she had so much alcohol was the time after she heard she would never dance professionally again. She became a binge drinker after that she used alcohol to numb the pain. But once she found out she was pregnant with Billy, her maternal instincts took over, and she only ever had the occasional glass of wine.

She needed coffee and lots of it; it was the only thing that would get her through the day.

Ryan was at the coffee station prepping for the morning crowd. He looked up at her, "Whoa Maise! I'm sorry to say it but you looking a little peaky today, what did you get up to last night? Maisey slumped onto a chair nearby and held her head in her hands.

"Don't go there Ryan, please tell me that there is coffee ready, I'm about to keel over right here." Ryan poured Maisey a coffee and handed it to her.

"Talking about peaky, what's wrong with you, you seem out of sorts this morn? Anything you want to share?" Maisey asked quietly.

"Naaah, nothing to worry yourself about." Answered Ryan he was wiping the surfaces down, he didn't want to meet Maisey's eye, she might be a bit off colour today, but she was still very perceptive.

"I can't believe it, look at her!" Maisey gestured towards the door, Breda had just arrived looking like she had a full eight hours sleep.

"If you want to know why I look like this ask Breda, she is responsible for my pain this morning."

Maisey climbed off the stool and walked towards the restrooms. Breda sauntered passed Ryan, "So, Breda I see you're trying to corrupt our Maisey into your wicked ways."

Breda shot Ryan a look of contempt, "Well my dear, you should know. We all have a level where we can be persuaded over to the dark side."

Ryan just grunted and turned around. He didn't feel like getting into it with the likes of Breda this morning.

She ventured on "Oh, by the way, are you not telling us something",

"What is it now Breda? I'm busy?" she smiled a cat-like smile.

"We all family here, surely you should share if you have news? Like a new girlfriend?"

Ryan looked at Breda suspiciously and shot back, "What the hell are you on about, are you still drunk from the last night?"

"Don't get tense with me, I'm just the messenger, some guy across the road gave this to me to give to you, it smells nice too".

Breda handed Ryan an envelope. Ryan snatched it out of her hand anxiously.

"He said to tell you it was a letter from your girlfriend".

Ryan's heart was beating fast; he ripped the envelope open, there was nothing in it, he leapt over the coffee station counter and ran towards Mickey.

Breda had never seen the likes of it before; Ryan jumping over the counter was an act of pure power, like a jaguar in the jungle. She really wanted to despise him, but it was difficult when he looked so darn good.

"Mick, I need a word", Ryan grabbed him by the arm and they went hurriedly to the office. "Victoria's in danger, she is in danger!" Ryan thrust the letter into Mickey's face.

"Calm down Ryan, how do you know this? Is this letter the only proof? Mickey looked down at the envelope; it was very generic, the writing on the envelope was addressed to Ryan. "It smells like her, the bastards have her I just know it!"

Ryan was pacing around the room, running his hands roughly through his jet-black hair. "The worst thing is, I don't have her phone number, and I don't even know where she lives?"

Just then there was a knock on the door, "Eh Mick", Maisey stepped into the office, "sorry to disturb, but there's a lady out here asking about one of our regulars. Would you talk to her? Ryan, please can you come back, I have coffee orders backing up."

Ryan looked up at her, his face was thunderous, but he managed to contain himself and he answered Maisey calmly.

"Just two secs, Maise, I have to sort something out with Mickey, it's crucial. Get Cormac behind the station he knows what to do."

Maisey was about to say something, but the urgency in Ryan's voice made her think twice. Mickey got up and said, "Let me go see what's happening out front. Do not do anything crazy just wait here."

He gestured for Ryan to remain calm. Ryan paced around the room some more, he felt out of control, he hated feeling this way; he could not believe that he had brought this on Victoria.

He couldn't stand around doing nothing, so he followed Mickey back into the Cafe. Mickey was speaking to a smallish woman with sandy blonde hair and glasses, she was neatly dressed in a grey business suit, almost something Victoria would wear. As he got near, he picked up the tail end of the conversation.

"I feel so silly going around and asking these questions, but I'm looking for a friend of mine, she comes here almost daily, I can't get hold of her and I was wondering if you had seen her today? She's tall, long brown hair, well-groomed, nose in her laptop?"

Ryan could not believe his luck; he knew this woman was referring to Victoria.

"Sorry to butt in like this, but are you looking for Victoria?" The woman looked confused, "Er, yes, Victoria Leeson. Was she in today? Ryan moved Liz by the arm to an empty table nearby, they both sat down.

"She hasn't been in today, but I did see her here last night."

Liz looked surprised, "Victoria was here last night?"

Ryan waved his hand and said irritably, "I need to know where Victoria lives. It's important!" Liz backed away slightly, this disarmingly handsome man had a dangerous edge to him. She answered carefully, "I'm sorry I'm not giving out my friend's personal information." Ryan swore under his breath.

"Look, the problem is that your friend could possibly be in danger, I need to find her to make sure she is fine."

It took every bit of Ryan's control not to shake Liz. Mickey could see that Ryan was about to lose his temper; he stepped in and calmly explained the situation to Liz.

"Victoria was here last night, but we received a disturbing note that makes us think that she might be in need of our help. We don't have time to get into the matter. Please, we just need her mobile number and her home address."

Something in the tone of Mickey's voice made Liz trust him.

"I really do not know what's going on here, but I'm going to give you Victoria's number, and I will be going with you to her house!"

Mickey and Ryan nodded in agreement. "Ryan, go get your car, I will let the others know you have to step out, they will know what to do".

Ryan turned to Liz, "I will meet you at the car park near the church in 5 minutes, are you driving?"

"Yes, I have my car".

CHAPTER 14

Ryan followed Liz's red Toyota Yaris in his black Land Rover. He believed in living life simply, but when it came to cars he would not compromise on style and comfort. After a few miles, Liz stopped outside a newly refurbished Georgian. The view of the beach was remarkable, whatever Victoria did for a living she was obviously good at it judging by the area she lived in and the size of her home.

The blinds of the house were still drawn; Liz opened the gate and walked up the front steps to knock on the door. Ryan followed closely; they all stood on the front steps looking awkwardly at each other. Liz knocked again; this time she felt more frantic, where the hell was Victoria?

Ryan was getting jumpy. He started thumping on the door frantically. "Victoria!" he was shouting, he didn't give a hoot about what the neighbors thought. He had to know if Victoria was fine. Still no answer.

"Liz, try her phone again." Ryan urged. Liz did what she was told, after a few seconds they heard a buzzing sound coming from the inside of Victoria's house.

"Oh My God! Her phone is on the house, but, where is she? Liz, do you have a key? We have to get in".

By this stage, Liz felt extremely concerned, she walked over to a Grecian looking urn that stood near the front door. The flowers billowing out of it were in full bloom, if the situation was not so serious she would have stopped and literally smelt the flowers. She stuck her hand around and fumbled in the plants and pulled out a key. Ryan looked sternly at her.

"I can't believe that people still do that in this day and age, how incredibly stupid can you ladies be, do you know how dangerous the world is? Hiding a key in the plant", Ryan shook his head in disbelief.

Liz suddenly felt very irritated by this gorgeous stranger and she shot back, "in case you have not noticed this is not the inner-city streets, this is a lovely neighborhood with good respectable people!"

"And that's exactly why you need to be more careful, this "lovely" little neighborhood contains goods and treasures of much value all the more reason for unsavory elements to pay you a visit".

Liz rolled her eyes at Ryan and unlocked the door.

The house was incredibly quiet, no sign of struggle or distress anywhere.

Ryan indicated towards the upstairs, "I will look up there you look down here". Liz was seriously getting tired of being bossed around by Ryan.

Ryan moved up the staircase. He was distracted by a sound coming from the room at the end of the corridor. So far, he was impressed with Victoria's decor style, simple, clean lines, and modern, but keeping with the traditional look of the house. The noise grew louder as he moved toward the end room. He quietly drew his gun from his jacket pocket, he pushed the door handle down and entered the room, the noise had stopped, and he realized it had come from the bathroom, he crept slowly to the bathroom door and with force he kicked the door open and pointed the gun into the room.

Maybe Victoria went home to see her Mam, she was under a lot of stress; Liz was downstairs in the kitchen trying to rationalize Victoria's disappearance. All of a sudden, she heard a blood-curdling scream from upstairs, her heart jumped into her throat and she ran upstairs.

"What the devil are you doing here?" screamed Victoria. She was standing outside her shower with little, but a very angry expression on her face.

Ryan was so taken back by the sight of Victoria's wet naked body he was rendered temporarily mute. Victoria hurriedly grabbed a towel from the rail and covered herself. Ryan was torn between wanting to scoop Victoria up into his arms and crushing her with relief that she was fine, but at the same time he wanted to scream at her for putting him through the hell he had been in all morning.

Just then Liz came bursting in.

She ran towards Victoria and embraced her, "I'm so glad you are fine, you gave us such a scare.

Victoria was just about to give out to Liz, but she looked down into her friend's eyes and saw genuine concern, Liz had tears in her eyes. Victoria calmly disentangled herself from Liz's grasp and she took a deep breath.

"Would somebody please tell me what you both are doing here" she suddenly became aware she was still in her towel, and under Ryan's close scrutiny. She pulled the towel closer to her body.

Liz suddenly aware of Victoria's lack of clothes ushered Ryan out of the room.

"I will explain while Victoria gets dressed, please go downstairs and maybe put on some coffee. Ryan was about to say something but thought better of it and stalked out of the room.

Victoria waited for the sound of Ryan going down the steps, "Just give me two seconds to throw something on and then I want a full explanation".

Liz moved to the window, "I think you are the one that needs to give an explanation, what is going on between you and Mr. Gorgeous? You really are a dark horse!"

Victoria now dressed in a pair of casual jeans and an emerald green ribbed tight-fitting jumper; gave Liz dagger looks.

"There is nothing going on between Ryan and me are you crazy?" Victoria was blushing from head to toe, she ran her fingers through her wet hair, and flopped herself down on the white ottoman at the foot of her large king-sized bed.

"I can't get into it now about Ryan; I just want to know why there was a party in my room that I didn't know I was invited to?"

Liz drew up the cream wing backed chair that had been next to the window, "I am kind of confused too, and it all started when I could not get hold of you on your mobile and house phone this morning. The first place I thought to go, and look is at the coffee shop you always go to, I asked one of the waitresses if they had seen you and she asked the owner. But all of a sudden, Ryan appeared and was asking all sorts of strange questions. To end the long story, we ended up here because apparently Ryan received some letter with information about you, I don't know you will have to ask him, I'm just glad that you are fine. In any case, why didn't you answer your phone or your door all this could have been avoided?" Liz said with irritation in her voice.

Victoria stood up and started pacing the room, "I had a really bad day yesterday, a bit of a crazy night and I just needed a little time without distraction, so I left my phone downstairs, took a sleeping pill and went to bed. With all that's going on, the last thing I wanted to do was check my phone messages."

They were distracted by a knock on the door, Victoria went over to open it, Ryan had two cups of coffee, the smell was heavenly, but what was more heavenly was the sight of him, she wanted to run her hands all over his muscled torso, he was so close she could see him draw breath. His presence was so disturbing, but in another way, she was truly relieved to see him.

"I thought you ladies could do with some coffee," he handed Victoria a cup of the steaming hot liquid, their fingers brushed slightly causing Victoria's breath to catch and she looked straight into Ryan's eyes, the message she read in his look was loud and clear, he was more than willing to take up where their antics of the night before had ended.

Victoria blushed, and quickly moved to the other side of the room. Liz looked on with curious interest, the electricity between Ryan and Victoria was ridiculous. She stood up and declined Ryan's offer for coffee.

"Ryan, you drink it. You look like you need it! I better head back to the office, Dermott has texted me three times already, I can't wait until you get back I could just hit his stupid face with my laptop every time he is in the room." Liz hugged Victoria and left.

CHAPTER 15

Maisey, was completely "done in" when her shift finished later that day, she wanted a hot bath and early night. She hoped that Billy would not be too difficult this evening, especially since he had not seen her since the night before. She would make him his favorite for tea, pork bangers with spring onion mash, and then they would settle in and watch a movie together. She picked up her handbag from her locker and headed for the door. "Goodnight, Mick, see ya in the morning".

"Erm, Maisey before you go can I ask you something?" Mickey became all awkward. Maisey had that uneasy feeling again.

"Sure Mick, what's up?" She asked hoping she sounded casual.

"I have this function. I have to go to, down in Cork and I was wondering," Maisey held her breath, please don't ask me to go with, she said silently to herself.

"If you would hold the fort for me while I was away? Ryan has some stuff going on, and I need a second in command that I can rely on." Mickey finished. Maisey was so relieved; she gave herself a start when she shouted her answer back at him.

"Of course, Mick, I would be happy to!"

"Thanks, Maise, I knew I could count on you!" Mickey walked towards Maisey and gave her an awkward embrace.

That uneasy feeling washed over Maisey again, why was Mickey hugging her? Was she right in her initial feeling that Mickey had feelings for her? She hoped it wasn't the case, she loved Mickey with all her heart as a father-figure. She would hate for anything to ruin that. But she suddenly realized that Mickey had entrusted her with the Cafe. She felt so proud of herself, she knew she could run the place with her eyes closed. The business course required actual practice in the business place, maybe she could use this time.

She felt quite excited as she walked towards the bus stop, it all seemed to be coming together for her, first her opportunity to study again, Billy making progress and now a chance to prove herself.
The bus stop was quite crowded, a queue of people started forming waiting to get onto the bus that had just stopped. Maisey took her place in the queue. While waiting for the people to get off the bus, suddenly Maisey was pushed forward. To stop herself from sprawling to the ground she stepped to the side, as she stepped, she accidentally trod all over a strange man getting off the bus. The man let out a yelp of pain and started hopping around on one leg. "Oh, my goodness, I am terribly sorry, but they pushed me from the back. " Maisey indicated to the queue of people behind her. The man mumbled something under his breath took one scathing look at Maisey and hobbled off in the opposite direction.
Maisey finally found her seat on the bus, but she couldn't help thinking about the rude and disturbing man who she had trod on. At least he could have said something, he looked as if he was about to strike her. She shuddered and rested her head against the window, at least the trip home to Blackrock was short.

LOVE'S LAST CUP OF COFFEE

***

Mickey was in his office; the cafe was quiet, and everybody had left for the night. He sat staring into space, he was grateful that he had such trustworthy people in his life; Ryan and Maisey were like family to him. Just then, his thoughts were disturbed by a knocking sound. Who the devil could that be at this hour? Mickey said to himself. He got up from his chair feeling very disgruntled. He got up slowly, wincing slightly as he straightened up. He walked over towards the door, when he reached the door he couldn't believe his eyes, he fumbled for the key to the door and shouted, "Aaron, what in all that's true and holy, are you doing here!"

CHAPTER 16

After Ryan left, Victoria had felt a renewed surge of energy. She had gone to gym and when she got back she had received a surprise phone call from Bruce McCarthy. She had agreed to meet him the next morning. She went to bed early in hope that the next day would bring her good news. After a restless night's sleep, she had a quick breakfast. She was on her way to Bruce McCarthy's office. He said he had something important to discuss with her.

After the antics of the past 48 hours she needed to focus on getting her life back on track. Ryan was a distraction. An understatement! The biggest distraction. When Liz had left them alone in her bedroom yesterday, it had been so awkward. She didn't know if she wanted to tackle him onto the bed and beg him to take her or high tail it out of there and keep running without looking back.

In the end, after an even more awkward silence, Ryan made the first move, he made her promise to be careful and then made some excuse and left.

This was the wrong time to become involved with someone, her focus should be on clearing her name and getting revenge on Dermott, but her mind was a foggy mess at the moment.

She felt so confused; she grabbed her biker jacket and headed out the door. It felt good to get back behind the wheel of her metallic baby blue Mini Cooper; she started the car and pulled off into the traffic.

Further down the road, a black SUV pulled out moments after her.

This damn traffic! Thought Victoria, Bruce Mc Cathy's office was all the way over across town, why hadn't she taken the motorway; she felt she had been on the road for hours. She looked in her rearview mirror and she noticed the same black SUV, which had been behind her 20 minutes ago had reappeared. She would have never noticed anything like this before, but with all the craziness lately she couldn't help but feel unnerved. Maybe she should let Ryan know. Before she could reach for her phone, the traffic started moving again, and she was forced to abandon her phone and drive on. She put on some music and sang away her troubles.

Finally, after being in traffic for an hour Victoria was seated across from Bruce in his comfortable wood paneled office.

"So, these documents prove that you have nothing to do with Dermott's dodgy dealings. He made the big mistake of signing off on these business lunches, which places him with the director of Steelcor's opposition on the day that the information was leaked about your involvement.

Bruce, leaned over his desk with his arms stretched forward and said, "Frankly, I thought Dermott was smarter than this, only an idiot would leave a paper trail when trying to frame someone else."

"So, does this mean I can get my job back and I am in the clear? I need to get back to work. The Steelcor deal was nearly signed and sealed." Victoria said hopefully, her hands were red and sore; she had been sitting and wringing them while Bruce was talking. "That's the good news. I spoke to your boss and sent over all the proof. He is ready to reinstate you and kick Dermott to the curb. I wanted to tell you myself, as I wanted to reassure you that the deal had not been compromised."

Victoria jumped up from her seat and ran over to Bruce's side of the desk. In the most uncharacteristic way, she reached over and gave him a hug out of gratitude. She pulled back when she realized what she had done.

"I'm sorry for that unprofessional display, but you have no idea what I have gone through this past week. I promise from now on I will revert back to the same no-nonsense solicitor you hired to do the job."

Bruce McCarthy let out a booming laugh; he was rather taken by surprise. Victoria was not one to display emotions, something had changed in her, maybe it was the threat of losing her livelihood, she appeared softer, not in the wimpy kind of way, but in a more human, more approachable way.

"Well that's reassuring, if I ever had to tell anyone what just happened now, they would think I was hitting the sauce."

Victoria laughed, said good-bye and left.

She felt as if she was walking on a cloud, she could get her life back; everything could go back to normal. But as she walked towards her car she had a nagging feeling that she might not want everything to go back to normal. Normal meant work 100% and definitely no Ryan. But did she want that? She reached into her bag for her keys, but never found them because all of a sudden, she was staring into a dark abyss.

∗∗

It took every inch of restraint in Ryan's body to leave Victoria yesterday. He could see the want in her eyes, but he could also see the mistrust and uncertainty. He had put her in so much danger; he needed to sort the situation out before anything seriously happened. He had called his security company as soon as he got back to the Café,' he needed to know that Victoria was safe, they had been tailing her since she left her house this morning. It was 13:15 he was a due an update at one.

What the hell was going on? He was getting impatient. He had left the coffee making duties to Cormac for the day; he couldn't focus on anything, but Victoria's safety. His phone buzzed in his pocket.

"Why the hell are you getting back to me so late," barked Ryan down the phone.

"Listen," said the voice on the other end of the line "I have just found Victoria's bag next her car, she is gone. And, another thing, there seems to be drops of blood on the parking lot floor."

CHAPTER 17

That morning had been a busy one in the Café, Maisey was sitting quietly in the back of the Café, she was on a break, she was still reeling from the chaos of the morning, and it had been hectic.

Without Ryan making coffee, she felt she had to work a bit harder to get the orders out, Cormac was great, but he didn't have the speed of Ryan. She looked into her handbag and took the manila envelope out. It was addressed to her; it displayed the stamp of the college she had applied to. She was so nervous; slowly with shaky hands she tore it open. "Dear Ms O'Brien, we are pleased to ......", She had got in, Maisey jumped up and let out a huge whoop, the Café was not very full, but the few customers still there turned to look at the distraction. Maisey rushed into Mickey's office, she couldn't wait to tell him the good news. "Mick, you will never believe…" she never finished her sentenced, because it wasn't Mick in his chair behind the desk. The coldest eyes of the bluest azure connected with hers, throwing her off.

"Excuse me, I don't think you should be back here, this is the manager's office." Maisey warned in an authoritative voice.

"Well, I think I am going to remain here, because my feet feel safe behind the desk, or are you going to come over here and jump all over them?" The cold eyes spoke, the voice almost as icy as the eyes.

Maisey could not believe her eyes and her bad luck, she suddenly realised this was the rude creature who almost assaulted her when she "accidently" stood on him. Ok, he didn't almost assault her, but the taciturn wuthering look could definitely be counted as hostile. Still holding Maisey's gaze, he got up and walked across the room. Maisey couldn't help but look at his tall and athletic frame; she shook her head and gained composure. "Regardless of what you think I'm going to do, I demand to know what you are doing back here?" That will teach him, who the hell did he think he was any way? She worked here and she will be managing the place soon, even if it's only for a week while Mickey was away. Before the tall intruder could answer, Mickey walked into the room, he looked at Maisey and looked at the stranger, a deep shade of red rushed over his face. "Aah, Maisey! I see you have already met my son, Aaron.

***

Ryan was in a panic. He had never felt so helpless before. He ran out of the Café. He didn't have time to tell Mickey, he got to his car and phoned his solicitor. He also made another phone call, he never thought he would ever have to dial this number, but he had no choice. "Shane, it's Ryan; I need your help, where can I meet you?" Ryan wrote the address down.

Shane "The Knuckle" Sweeney, otherwise known as Shane Sweeney, ran in the same gang as Ryan many years back. Lucky for Shane when Ryan's gang was bust, he had been laid up in hospital with a broken leg. Shane stuck to the gang life, and over the years they both had lost touch, especially since Ryan had betrayed his fellow gang members.

Ryan drove like a maniac to an industrial side of town, down a narrow alley way with warehousing on each side. He parked his car and walked over to a doorway cut into the large corrugated steel gate. The alley smelt faintly like old alcohol and urine; litter sat lazily in the street.

Ryan opened the makeshift door, it led into another narrow alley. Ryan walked down the path, he was fully aware that Shane could have sold him out and that he could be entering into a trap, he felt his left pocket, he had come prepared. He could feel the outline of the gun and somehow this gave him some comfort. Trap or no trap he needed to do this it was the only way he could get to Victoria and get her to safety.

Shane watched Ryan from his office window, walking down the path towards the door, he had to admire him. He still had that cocky air of someone who just didn't give a shit. Ryan had aged well. Unlike him, I suppose doing what he did he would look older more lined, gang life wasn't for wimps.

Shane always had a soft spot for Ryan, believing that if he ever had the moxy to do what Ryan did he would have given the crime life up ages ago. But regardless of how he felt personally, business was business and he had to get on and do his.

Ryan walked into what he thought was a warehouse, which he realised, was actually the back entrance of a pub, empty draught kegs lined up against the wall. Two rough looking men appeared in front of him, they patted him down and removed his weapon, and they gestured towards the steps. Ryan drew in a hard breathe, he had no choice but to follow them. The staircase made creaky noises, definitely not made for stealth. The two men indicated for Ryan to go through a door at the top of the steps, he walked into the room and they closed the door behind him.

The office was dark and dingy, heavy green velvet curtains hung on the windows adding to the drama of the room. A large black leather couch lined the one wall. A dark wooden desk took up the middle of the room.

Behind it sat Shane; he was staring at Ryan waiting for him to make the first move. Ryan knew this was Shane's thing; he was good at unnerving people by just looking at them. Ryan also knew Shane's name "The Knuckle" was given to him for a reason. Before Shane moved up the ranks he was used as an "intimidator," often having to use his knuckles to get what was needed.

Ryan stood firm and began the exchange.

"Something tells me you know exactly why I am here, but I am not going to mess around with you, I need to get a message to Jack, he has something of mine and I want it back!"

Shane tapped his thick, rough index finger on the desktop.

"Let's take this down a notch; you were the one who called me, what makes you think I know what you are on about?"

"Shane don't act dumb with me, you would have phoned Jack as soon as the call ended with me, there was no way you would meet with me without him knowing".

Shane took a deep breath in and said, "So, let me get this right, so what you are saying is that I am loyal and I would never sell my kin out, rat them out to the Garda".

Ryan knew his past would come up, but he was ready for it.

"I'm not here for a trip down memory lane, Shane. Victoria has nothing to do with this, if Jack has an issue with me, then let him take it up with me and me alone."

"Tell Jack I will meet him but only on the condition that Victoria is not harmed".

"I'm glad you said that Ryan, because I wasn't in the mood to "convince" you, despite what I have to do here, I remember all the times you protected me and you never named me as one of the gang members in Jack's trial. That is the only reason why you are not sitting at the bottom of the canals."

Ryan nodded an understanding, "Let Jack know what we agreed to and make sure he doesn't even make a scratch on Victoria, or he will see himself at the bottom of the canals" warned Ryan.

CHAPTER 18

Maisey could feel her cheeks burning, "I wouldn't say we have formally met yet, but I will leave you two alone to talk."

Maisey almost ran out of the room, she stood in the passage outside of the office and lent her shoulder against the cool of the wall, why was she feeling so embarrassed, it should be that rude Aaron who should be feeling humiliated. She fanned herself with her docket book. She was interrupted by Mickey coming out of the room.

"Maisey, I am glad you are still here, was there something you needed me for? You ran out of there so fast you left this envelope."

"Oh, ehm, I just wanted to let you know I was accepted to do the course".

Mickey clapped his hands together and enveloped Maisey into a bear hug, with all that had happened lately Maisey would have felt uncomfortable with Mickey's display of affection, but somehow the hug was genuine and extremely comforting.

She found herself hugging Mickey back, the excitement about receiving good news returned and she was gushing like a school girl. The moment did not last forever, they heard someone clear their throat behind them and they quickly drew apart, causing that awkward feeling to return.

Maisey indicated towards the Café and said. "Best I get back, or else Breda will be giving out until the cows come home."

Mickey nodded and headed back to the office. As Maisey was about to leave, Aaron grabbed her by the arm and pulled her slightly roughly to one side and whispered in her ear.

"I know what you are up to, and I am not going to let you pull one over on my father, fluttering your eyelashes, flicking your silky hair, he is a vulnerable old man who has been through a lot." He dropped her arm and marched back into the office.

Maisey was stunned, before she could say anything he was gone. She could not believe the audacity of that man, how dare he, she didn't even know what he was talking about. She actually felt physically sick. She was so upset, she almost ran after him, but she knew if she started at him, he was with Mickey and maybe that's what he wanted.

She took herself off the ladies room to splash water on her face and gain composure.

When she came out of the bathroom, the Café was teaming with customers, Breda shot her a look of pure fire. Oh great! Just what I need, an afternoon with Breda on my case.

***

Victoria, tried to move her arms, her eyes were sore and her vision blurry. Where the hell was she? And what was going on? She tried to move again, but her head was pounding. She reached to brush her hair away from her face, but she found half the strands sticking to the side of her face. Why was her hair so dry and crusty? She shook her head to try clear her vision, which was now slowly returning.

Everything had a fuzzy edge, even the cloud she was looking through; she could see she wasn't exactly in the Merrion. The room was dark, the blinds were drawn, it was empty except for the formally beige ratty old sofa she had been sitting on, and it had certainly seen better days.

Her body felt heavy, if she could just make it over to the door, maybe she could see where she was. She slowly got to her feet, her head spinning making her promptly sit down. After a few deep breaths she tried again, she managed to stand upright and shuffle one foot at a time to towards the door, she noticed that she was barefoot. What a bloody cheek! She didn't know if she was angrier over losing her expensive black Valentino T-bar pumps, or the fact that she had been kidnapped and somebody had put her in a state of undress while she was unconscious.

Her heart started pumping as the realisation of her situation crept over her like a wave of nausea. Still shuffling towards the door, she noticed the door handle had been removed; she was well and truly stuck. Maybe the windows? She shuffled over to the window, but they wouldn't budge. She became frantic and started pulling on the blinds, nothing she did helped, the blinds were made out of strong wood, all she got for her efforts was a splinter in her finger.

Sucking on the forefinger that now had a piece of wood stuck in it, she wondered who would want to hurt her? It must be the people Ryan was talking about, but why her? She wasn't involved with Ryan. It's not like she was his girlfriend or anything? For fecks sake! If this what happens because she shared one steamy session with Ryan, what would have happened if they actually had sex?

All her noise must have caused a disturbance, because she heard footsteps, coming towards the door; she felt scared and moved as quickly as she could to get back over to the dilapidated sofa in the corner. The door opened slowly, expecting to see some overgrown face basher with half a brain, she almost fell off the sofa when she saw who it was and shouted in surprise, "You bastard!"

CHAPTER 19

Victoria felt sick to her stomach; she couldn't believe Dermott was standing in front of her. "Hello Vicky, are you comfortable?"

Victoria scrambled up off the sofa to get some distance between herself and Dermott.

"I can't believe you would do this to me! I knew you were a creep, but I didn't know you were a kidnapper too, have you been fired yet? The Gardaí should be here soon to arrest you; Bruce McCarthy cleared everything this morning".

Dermott let out a rumbling laugh, he walked over and sat on the arm of the sofa.

"Victoria you are so trusting, are you really that stupid not to know that Bruce McCarthy has been part of this from the beginning?"

"You are lying!" Victoria retorted, she would not let Dermott get into her head.

She moved towards him, quicker now, her drowsiness had worn off, "then tell me one thing, why is that if he was part of the deal, would he warn me about you?" Dermott's sickly smirk disappeared off his face, but only for a moment before the fake smile returned.

"That was part of the whole act, how do you think we could get him to get you to his office?" Victoria swore under breath, turned her back to him, she refused to believe him. She knew Bruce McCarthy was a good man.

There was a knock at the door, and the door opened slightly, Victoria could not see who it was but Dermott turned to her.

"Please excuse me for a second I am just going to take care of something." He closed the door behind him, Victoria heard two sets of voices, one obviously Dermott's and the other she did not recognise, and she crept over to the door and put her ear against it. She could barely make out the words, but one word was clear, she heard the unknown man say something about "it's going to be fun and games when Ryan arrives", and then afterwards she heard the men break into guffaws and snickers.

Victoria heard Dermott at the door she backed away and went and sat on the sofa, Dermott stuck his head in.

"I need to be somewhere, if I was you Vicky, I would use this time to think about things, and once you have calmed down, we could come to some "amicable" agreement." Victoria jumped up.

"Dermott you cannot leave me here! How long are you going to keep me here? There will be people looking for me! this is ridiculous! Who do you think you are, a member of the mob?" Victoria said mockingly. Dermott, scowled he was just about to say something, but thought twice about it, he closed and locked the door.

Victoria felt deflated, she had never felt so lost and alone before, why would Dermott be doing this to her, she had never done anything to purposely hurt him?

She went over to a little table at the end of the room; there was bottled water and a few packets of crisps. She wanted to refuse to eat anything, they offered but she thought she might need her strength later. She drank a whole bottle of water in three long gulps and finished two packets of crisps, sour cream and onion flavour, the last thing she needed to worry about was how fresh her breath smelt. The most important thing was to keep calm, and try think of some way out of this mess.

CHAPTER 20

"You have to go the Garda with this one Ryan; you cannot take on Jack by yourself. Has he contacted you?"

Mick and Ryan were in the Café' office, Ryan got up to pour their evening whisky, with a wave of his hand Mickey declined. Taken a little back Ryan put the glass back down on the drinks tray, it was still a little early; maybe he would change his mind later.

"Mickey, I cannot go the Garda, the instructions were that if the authorities were notified they would know, and Victoria would become a distant memory."

"Ryan, they make threats all the time, but this is serious, Jack needs to be put out of commission permanently."

"He is out of commission. As far as I know, he is still locked up. No, someone is acting as his proxy, and they have decided to settle old scores."

Mickey coughed, "Did Shane tell you anything? After all you did save his hide all those years back."

Ryan shook his head, "According to Shane, the fact that he didn't kill me on the spot was pay back enough; he is so far up Jack's arse he can't see the sun."

Ryan jumped up from the desk, "I am going out of my mind, I cannot wait, I need to do something, and I feel like such an eejit for putting her in this position".

Mickey got up out of the chair, but was suddenly overcome by a dizzy spell; he wavered and promptly sat back down again. Ryan rushed over to his side, "Mickey are you okay?" Mickey caught his breath and answered slowly, "I'm grand, Ryan, just got up a little too quickly, that's all."

Ryan looked at Mickey; he looked fine, a bit pale maybe? He had lost a lost a bit of weight recently, but that could be due to the new diet he was on. He was digressing, Mickey was fine. Ryan felt nervous, he had yet to hear back from Shane, and surely they were going to make an arrangement point, him in exchange for Victoria. His thoughts were disturbed by the sound of his mobile buzzing in his pocket. He drew in a deep breath and answered it. "Shane, any news yet?" He nodded his head. "Not sure if the Café is the best place, it must be after closing time" He waited for a reply on the other end. "See you tonight at 10pm". He ended the call and felt his heart beat accelerate, tonight was the night where he finally stopped running and sorted out this mess once and for all.

***

"Breda, Cormac, I just need to tell you that Maisey will be in charge for the next week, I have some business in Cork; and Breda before you ask, yes. I have some extra help coming in so you won't be taking on all the tables yourself." Maisey could see the looks Breda was giving her, but she didn't care, Mickey had trusted her enough to run everything while he was away. Breda was never one to give up on an opportunity to say something, "So, where's lover boy Ryan going to be?" "Not that it's any of your business Breda; he needs some time off to sort out some personal issues." Mickey retorted. "Which means Cormac you are on fulltime coffee duty."

Mickey nodded, indicating the impromptu meeting had reached its end. He shuffled back slowly to towards his office.

When he was out of earshot Breda spoke up, "If you ask me, I think Mickey is hitting the bottle again. He probably is going to some drying out clinic. He hasn't been right for a few months now." Maisey could not believe the absolute drivel coming from Breda's mouth, she shot back, "Breda, we did not ask you anyway and would you kindly keep your half-baked notions to yourself!" Maisey felt so angry with her, she honestly could have clobbered her with a tray.

"Say what you want, Maisey, but there is definitely something off with him." With that, Breda flounced off to deliver her food orders from the kitchen. Breda really was a nasty piece of work, after all the shite Mickey had to put up with from her. She was an ungrateful brat, who in actual fact did not need to work at all. You would never say it if you had to lay eyes on her ,but she was a private school princess.

"Come on Maisey, old girl, you better get back to work, unlike Breda you do need to work for a living" she said to herself.

CHAPTER 21

Victoria tried to judge what the time was, she had no clue how long she had been in the room for. She could not go by the light outside, it was summer and the sun still seemed high up in the sky, it could be five o'clock or eight o'clock. Surely someone would be looking for her. She realised that not many people would even notice if she was missing. She did the obligatory phone call home once a week, where she would discuss the same topics in the same sequence.

Her mother would first ask about her job, she never went into too many details, then her mother would discuss the latest gossip in the village, and they would say goodbye until the next conversation. Even though she did not have a close relationship with her parents, she looked after them financially. Her parents had moved off the small farm and moved to the neighbouring village where Victoria had bought them a comfortable three bedroomed cottage. Her dad had been sober for many years, he managed to keep down the same job for the past ten years and both parents seemed happy.

Victoria also made sure any money she sent home went straight into an account controlled by her mother, even though her dad was on the straight and narrow she didn't want put temptation in his way.

Being holed up in a small room all day gave Victoria time to think, all she could do was think, it had been a long time when she was forced to sit and reflect. Liz would be worried, surely? Not many other people she could think of who would care that she was missing. Which brought Victoria to the one person who she was trying not to think about, the one person who no matter what she did, she couldn't get out of her mind? She had thought about the night when Ryan had kissed her, over and over. What would have happened had they not been interrupted? She shuddered, she couldn't believe she was even thinking these thoughts at time like this, but it seemed the only thing keeping her together.

She felt someone tugging at her, "wake up sleepy head, it's time to go" the voice was sinister and belonged to some hairy armed brute with one missing tooth.

She pushed his arm away and managed to drag herself into a standing position. Her limbs felt heavy and her brain was foggy, clearly they had put something in the water. She attempted to look down at her clothes, she resembled something from the bottom of her laundry basket all rumpled. She tried to pull at the creases.

Mr Toothy laughed "No need to make an effort on my account," and he laughed and nudged his equally brawny, brainless accomplice.

They hauled Victoria down the stairs. She was drained of energy and almost welcomed being semi-carried to the luxury dark sedan waiting with the door wide open.

It took a while before Victoria's eyes to adjust, the sun had dropped in the sky and a dusky haze was settling over the city, which brought with it a chilly wind.

Victoria got in the car and rubbed her arms. Her body sank down into the soft leather of the car seats, whoever owned the car had expensive taste. Anxiety began to build. Where were they taking her? Dermott was such a sleazy character, who knew who he was mixed up with. And, by the looks of things, these were the kind of people that could make other people disappear, permanently. Not for the first time that day did Victoria feel a chill of dread run down her spine. She wrapped her arms tighter around her body, and continued to stare out of the heavily tinted car window.

CHAPTER 22

The afternoon trade had dwindled and only one table was still occupied. Ryan found it very difficult to concentrate. He had spent most of the afternoon with the Gardaí. He was so worried about being followed so he met with Inspector O'Connor in an unmarked office just outside the city centre. Eammon O'Connor had been part of Ryan's original case against Jack Mulligan.

"Oh, you are still here?" Maisey asked as she came into the room. She had handed the last table their bill and walked over to Ryan. He tried to smile at her, but he couldn't force one out.

"Are you okay? You have been cagey since this morning?" Maisey leaned in across the counter. Ryan sighed and made as though he was wiping down the machines.

"I'm fine, Maise. Just some personal issues to deal with, but by tomorrow it should be all sorted out." This only made Maisey more suspicious about Ryan's behaviour. But by the look on his face, she decided not to press further.

"Why don't you go on home, I will lock up tonight .I am sure Billy would love that." Ryan wanted to get Maisey away from the Café', he did not need any more innocent people getting hurt.

"If you are sure, it would be lovely to get back early for a change." Ryan nodded and went back to pretend cleaning of the machines. Maisey let the last customers out of the shop and changed the door sign to "Closed".

Something very strange was going here, she felt it in her bones. Ryan was all jittery, and Mickey had evaded any kind of direct answer to her earlier questions about the situation. She grabbed her coat and purse and left.

CHAPTER 23

The early summer light was finally beginning to dip; it was 9:45 pm. Ryan had been pacing around the Café for the past hour. He had successfully ejected all persons out of the building. He felt his back pocket for his gun; he had forgotten he had hidden it away as they were bound to check him for weapons. He shuddered to think what condition Victoria would be in when he saw her, but knew that they wouldn't risk harming her if they had a perfect opportunity to finally get at him. Maisey was safely at home with her son, and he had sent Mickey and Aaron off to have dinner at the pub down the road.

He heard a faint knocking sound on the window. He walked slowly to the window and peaked out. It was Shane. He could make out that a black luxury sedan had parked outside the Café'.

Ryan went to unlock the door. Three heavy duty thug-like men pushed their way through the door, one roughly bumped passed Ryan with his shoulder. The same one patted Ryan down, checking for weapons and listening devices. It was not a pleasant experience been frisked by a 6.5 foot tall, hairy, tattooed thug, who frankly could have used a breath mint. Ryan's first instinct was to react with his fists, but he kept thinking about Victoria, he wasn't prepared to let his pride get in the way of her safety. He straightened out his shirt.

"Are you alone? barked Shane.

"Yes", Ryan answered through his teeth.

"Jamey, go check round back, we were told not to trust this feller". Another gangster oaf, who was equally as grotesque as the others, moved around the café in attempt to look for potential witnesses.

"Where is Victoria? She is supposed to be here, I have done everything you asked of me". Ryan asked Shane, he was clearly the one who seemed to be in charge.

"Keep yer hair on, she will be here in time", he sneered.

He gestured for the two other men; they huddled together and seemed to be holding some in depth discussion. Suddenly Shane's phone rang, he answered and listened intently, and he then gravelled out some sort of affirmation and gestured for the other two to go outside. Shane then stood and watched Ryan. To show Ryan he meant business, every now and then he would lift his jacket back to reveal a shiny gun. Ryan had planned ahead and had hidden his gun in the overflow section of the coffee machine. He managed to stash it there before he opened the door. He was back there now waiting for them to make the next move.

The other two gangsters knocked on the door, Shane let them in, and to Ryan's relief they had Victoria between them. He could see how exhausted she looked, but seemed unharmed. His heart swelled with relief at the sight of her.

Victoria looked up; her eyes had to adjust to the dark lighting in the Café. Her eyes focused on Ryan and a flicker of hope sparked inside. The whole day had felt surreal to her, like it was not happening to her. Now, she felt the full impact of the situation she had found herself in.

"Victoria, are you okay?" Ryan shouted across the room to her.

"Shut yer gobs, no talking to each other. Do you hear me?" said

Shane in a threatening tone.

They moved Victoria to a table close to the kitchen; Ryan was still behind the counter next to the coffee machines. He longed to smash all these assholes, pick up Victoria and carry her out of here.

There was a commotion coming from the back of the Café, obviously they had gained access through the back too. Just then, everybody went dead still and turned to see who had just entered through the front door.

CHAPTER 24

"Mick, what are you doing here, you shouldn't be here!" Ryan was shocked; the last thing he wanted was Mick to get hurt.

"Ol Mick is here to see me", said a voice emerging from the dark. Ryan's blood ran cold. It couldn't be him.

"I thought you were in prison?" Ryan shouted. Jack Sullivan let out a malicious laugh, "Ryan, that was always your problem, you think too much. Now all that thinking has landed you and your friends here." Jack made a sweeping gesture with his hands.

"You should have just kept your mouth shut, and our business to yourself in the first place."

Ryan looked around; Victoria stood shivering in the corner, now Mick was here too. Ryan walked towards Jack, he could see him better now, and time had not been kind to him in prison. His skin was ruddy and puffy, his hair once lush and a deep reddy-brown was now thin and straggly, peppered with a dirty grey.

"You have me now, let the others go, we can end this all tonight." Jack let out another bone-chilling laugh.

"Do you really think that it's going to be that simple, I have been wasting away cleaning toilets, staring at the same four walls for years all because of you, my wife divorced me, and my kids want nothing to do with me. Only my boys stuck my side".

Jack stepped forward into the light, he had something shiny in his hand, and before Ryan could react Jack drew his gun up and pointed towards Ryan and pulled the trigger. Ryan heard two popping sounds, expecting to feel an impact he saw another flash and suddenly it was all over, Mickey and Jack lay motionless on the ground.

Suddenly, the noise of sirens in the distance broke the silence. The men who were holding Victoria were in a panic, stuck between wanting to flee or to pick Jack up.

But sense prevailed, and they fled through the back entrance. Ryan, fell to his knees next to Mick. He could see blood trickling from his mouth. He tried frantically to find a pulse, but he was gone.

Victoria stood rooted to the spot; she couldn't believe what had happened. She looked at Ryan trying to revive Mick, she saw the emotions and pain, and something clicked inside of her. She ran over to Ryan, who by then, was being restrained by the police. She touched his shoulder; he stopped and looked up at her. She held her hand out to him and without question he took it.

CHAPTER 25

Nothing seemed real and the drive to her house felt like a thousand miles away. Victoria did not know how she found the strength to get Ryan into the car and drive him to her house.

Since Mickey's shooting, he had not said one word. They declined medical attention. Eammon O'Connor had offered to drive them both, but they both declined. They had to report to their local Garda Station in the morning to give statements about the event.

Victoria didn't know why she was taking Ryan back to her house; all she knew was that he could not be alone in his current state.

He looked completely heart-broken. She unlocked her front door and led him in by the hand. Neither had eaten, nor had anything to drink. She tried to offer Ryan something, but he stopped her mid-sentence.

Ryan took hold of Victoria's hand and led her upstairs to her bedroom. Once there, Ryan spoke for the first time his voice had a slight wobble to it.

"I still have Mickey's blood all over my shirt!" he gestured to the red stains, now deeply ingrained in the fabric. Victoria's eyes welled with tears; she moved closer to Ryan and began to slowly unbutton his shirt, one button at a time. She peeled it over his strong, muscled shoulders and let it fall to the floor. She then went to work on his trousers, unzipping them smoothly; she kneeled down and tugged them down his sculpted thighs and calves. He was now standing in his underwear.

Ryan then lifted Victoria's camisole over her head, she was wearing a white see-through lacy bra, and her pert, aroused nipples peaked through the material. He felt his erection harden, he hooked his fingers in her trousers and pulled her closer. He undid the buttons and the trousers fell to the floor. He stood back and marveled at the sheer beauty of her body, he longed to pull down the matching white lacy panties. Victoria then steered him into the bathroom, where she proceeded to discard both her bra and pants.

She reached into the shower and turned on the taps. Ryan stripped off his last layer and quickly moved towards Victoria and picked her up against his body. Their bodies melted into each other and the sheer heat consumed them. Ryan could not stand it anymore, he kissed Victoria's sumptuous lips, lightly at first, but he could feel her responding hungrily to him.

Their kiss deepened and intensified, Victoria flicked her tongue against his, which ignited more desire deep into her belly. Ryan pulled away slightly and set Victoria down; he looked deep into her eyes and asked.

"Would you please shower with me?" Victoria nodded and they both climbed into the already running shower, Victoria began to lather soap onto Ryan's arms and chest, she moved lower and ran her hands expertly over his toned stomach. She reached lower and encircled her hands around his large erect member; she moved her hands up and down the shaft, causing Ryan to groan with pleasure.

Before he lost control, he moved Victoria's hands and he pinned them above her head with one hand against the wall of the shower, he had been waiting such a long time to be with her he was going to take in every single second.

He kissed her neck lightly, his took the palm of his other hand and slightly rubbed her nipples, Victoria arched her back pushing her breasts closer to his mouth. He drew in one nipple to his mouth and circled it with his tongue making flicking motions. He let go of her hands and while he was working her nipples with his tongue and fingers, he moved lower and found her soft fleshy mound, he skillfully massaged her until she started moaning with pleasure. She gripped his hair roughly while he brought her to a deafening crescendo. Victoria had never been pleasured in this way, felt her limbs shake and tremble.

Ryan turned the running water off and picked her up out of the shower, he took two big fluffy towels off the shelf and proceeded to dry off first Victoria then himself. He then led her to the bed. Victoria now feeling fully recovered from her shower lay down on the bed and pulled Ryan on top of her.

Ryan could no longer hold back asked, "Do you have protection?"

Victoria nodded and gestured towards a drawer next to her bed. Ryan sat up and removed the packaging, Victoria watched him pull the sheath over his erection, she wanted him so badly, she swung her legs over him and straddled him, and she moved herself onto his erect penis and began to move up and down. Ryan moved his hips to meet hers and soon they were building a matching rhythm, Ryan barely held on until he heard Victoria cry and suddenly he let go and let the crashing waves descend on both of them.

CHAPTER 26

Maisey wanted to get into work early, it was always good to start the day early, and you missed the morning rush for a seat on the bus. Maisey got off the bus and walked across the road towards Café de Maison.

As she drew nearer, she saw the front door was taped up with yellow crime scene tape and the Gardaí were swarming around the place. A chill of dread went down her spine, she spotted Aaron speaking to one of the officers, he looked up and he was as white as a sheet.

She ran over towards him. "Aaron, what has happened, where are Mickey and Ryan?" Aaron turned to her, his face wet with tears. Maisey placed her hand on his shoulder and quietly urged him to speak. Aaron wiped the tears away with the back of his hand and quickly shrugged Maisey's hand from his shoulder.

"It's Mickey, my Dad, he's dead!" Maisey felt her legs go weak, her stomach churned, and her mind tried to reason with this shocking news.

"How, when?" was all she could get out. Aaron was about to explain when they heard screaming and crying from behind them, it was Breda.

"Oh Crap!" whispered Aaron under his breath. "That's all we need." He went over to Breda who now was being consoled by Cormac, who was looking extremely confused. Aaron gestured for Maisey to come over. "I can only explain this once, so let's go upstairs to the apartment."

Once upstairs, Cormac did what he knew best and made them coffee. Then all four sat around the small kitchen table.

They sat in silence for a long time as the magnitude of what had happened washed over them. Breda had eventually stopped blubbering. Maisey felt numb, she wasn't ready to believe that Mickey was gone. Aaron got up and began to relate the details of the previous night's events.

"I always knew Ryan was shady" spat Breda, "Now, he has gone and had Mickey killed. The bastard! And, where is he anyway? He is not here to pick up the pieces and explain himself."

Maisey felt angry but decided giving out to Breda would be ill-timed and disrespectful to Mickey. When all this is over she is going to have it out with her once and for all.

"Okay besides all that, why was Victoria there? What was her involvement in all this?" asked Maisey, still unsure of all the details.

"Apparently, she was used as some sort of leverage against Ryan; they kidnapped her and held her hostage."

"Ooh, the bastards!" exclaimed Maisey, "No wonder Ryan was so at odds, I put it down to him just been moody."

"But I still don't get, why Ryan was involved with those men, what were they doing in the Café," asked Breda.

"I don't have those answers yet, Breda, but I am determined to find out why my father was in the line of fire!"

Aaron looked weary; Maisey could see that he was tired. "Cormac, Breda let's go. I am sure Aaron has a lot to deal with."

Breda was about to protest, but the look on Maisey's face she decided against it. This time Aaron looked at Maisey with gratitude, it was the first the time he didn't look at her with contempt. The change made him look different, softer, almost.

They all got up from the table; Cormac patted Aaron on the shoulder and left with Breda in his wake.

Maisey hung back a bit, "Please let me know if there is anything I can do to help you?" Whatever she had seen in Aaron's eyes just moments before had disappeared and the same icy steel look had returned.

"I think you have helped yourself for long enough." Maisey felt as if she had been physically struck, she would never understand why Aaron mistrusted her so.

"Aaron, I am not sure what I ever did to you, but I know you are hurting now." With those last words she left, what she did not see was Aaron crumple to the floor in a flood of tears as the grief for his father took hold of him.

CHAPTER 27

The sun streamed into Victoria's bedroom, the warm rays touching the bottom of the bed. Ryan had been awake for over an hour, but didn't have the heart to wake Victoria, who was lying across his chest. She was exhausted from her ordeal with Jack's gang and it didn't help that they had made love twice during the night. He felt himself harden at the memory.

Victoria started to stir, the movement of her naked body against his was arousing, the sexual chemistry between them was like nothing he had ever experienced. He knew though it wasn't just sex, he was emotionally involved with her too.

Victoria opened her eyes and stretched lazily. "Good morning." She said shyly.

"Good morning to you too" he replied. He caught sight of her beautiful creamy breasts, it was too much for him, and he slid on top of her.

"Mm, I could get use to waking up like this in the morning," said Victoria cheekily and gripped his buttocks with both hands. They both were highly aroused, Victoria put her hand down to guide him into her. She wrapped her legs around him and pushed him deep inside her. Their lovemaking was urgent and they both within seconds could feel the buildup and climaxed quickly.

After a few minutes of heart rates now normalising, Ryan sat up suddenly and moved to the edge of the bed. The memories he had been trying to push back came at him with a force.

"Ryan?" Victoria asked. "Mickey's dead, Victoria, and it's all my fault." He put his head in hands, he got up from the edge of the bed, and he threw a towel around his waist and stood looking out of the window. Victoria did not know what to make of the sudden change in him.

"Mickey decided on his own to be there, you never asked him to be there and you certainly did not pull the trigger, don't you see it's not your fault," pointed out Victoria.

Ryan shook his head, "Don't you see? All of this is my fault! Mickey would still be alive if it wasn't for me. You would not have been kidnapped, if it was not for me. All of it is my fault!" Ryan was on a rant, his guilt and grief overtaking him. He started getting dressed; he flung on his clothes.

Victoria jumped out of bed and rushed to his side.

"Ryan, stop! Just stop for a moment! There is nothing you can do now, please calm down and let's talk about this."

"There's nothing to talk about, I am responsible for Mickey's death and that's it."

At this stage, Ryan was fully dressed and was pulling on his coat.

"Listen to me" urged Victoria, "You have lost someone close to you; you are not thinking rationally, just stay here with me, have some breakfast and we will deal with this together." Victoria took a deep breath and finished. "Did last night and this morning mean anything to you?" Her voice wavered.

Ryan looked at Victoria; he could see the hurt in her eyes.

"It's best if you don't get mixed up with me, I am not good for you,

you can do so much better. You need to be with someone good, someone without a past. Just know that last night with you meant more to me than you will ever realise. Good bye Victoria." He turned and left.

Victoria was overcome with emotion; she stormed down the stairs after him, still naked.

"I don't care what you are going through, Ryan; you are a bastard! A bastard!"

But it was no use the front door had slammed, and Victoria was left at the bottom of the stairs alone. She sat on the bottom step and hugged her arms around her legs, tears streaming down her face. Victoria could not believe what had just happened, the night with Ryan was the most beautiful and sensual night she had ever spent with anyone. They were so connected, mentally, emotionally, and of course, physically. She knew from the moment their bodies touched that she was falling in love with him. The elation she had felt this morning had rapidly been replaced with loss. She came to the sickening realization that Ryan had used her to block the memories of Mickey's death, and now she was all alone, again.

CHAPTER 28

When Ryan left Victoria's he walked for miles, not caring where he was going but he soon realised that he needed to get home, there was so much to sort out. He flagged a taxi down and climbed into the vehicle. Once back home, he took out his mobile phone, the battery was flat, so he set to charge. He paced around his kitchen, he could not sit still, he knew if he sat down the images of Mickey being shot, and the disappointment and hurt on Victoria's face would come back to haunt him.

His thoughts were disturbed by the ringing of his phone, the caller ID showed the Café. He felt sick, who would be calling him from there. He took a breath and answered.

"Thank God you answered. Ryan, where the hell have you been?" It was Aaron, Mickey's son.

"Aaron, I was just about to call you, I want to say…." He paused, he could not bring himself to offer his condolences, and it would sound hollow and make it all too real.

"I know Ryan, I feel the same way, would you come down to the Café, and we need to talk?"

"Sure, of course, what time must I meet you there? "Does three-thirty suit you?"

"Sure, see you then." Ryan had not even hung up yet when the phone went again, this time it was the Gardaí they wanted him to come down the station to give a statement. He arranged a time to meet them and decided he needed a good cup of coffee.

***

After two gruelling hours at the Garda station, Ryan made his way to the Café, he wasn't sure he could go back inside. By now, all the hype had simmered down and only one uniformed officer was visible. He opened the door and went in. Maisey was sitting at a table in the corner drinking coffee. Aaron was nowhere to be seen. When Maisey saw Ryan, she leapt out of her chair and threw her arms around him. Somehow seeing Maisey there comforted him and it felt natural. He hugged her close, her tears fell against his shoulder and he felt the tears in his eyes. They stayed like that for a long time, locked in grief.

It was Aaron's sudden arrival that broke them apart.

"I know this is difficult, but I came across a letter from my father, he wrote it early in the evening before he died."

Ryan and Maisey looked confused.

"What do you mean Aaron, how could he have known he would die?"

"Just read the letter, Ryan. It explains everything," Aaron handed him the letter. He took the letter with slightly trembling fingers; he cleared his throat and began to read out loud:

"My Dear Children (Aaron, Ryan and Maisey)

If you are reading this letter, than you know where I am. Please don't be sad this was my destiny.

It is difficult to explain but here goes. Ryan, I do not want you to blame yourself for what happens to me, it is going to happen anyway. What I mean is that I am sick, and there is nothing left that anyone can do medically. The doctors have given me weeks, so instead of trying to fill a lifetime of experiences into the next few weeks, I have decided to give the people I love a lifetime of love, and the ability to have new experiences without worry or looking over their shoulders. I am doing this so we all can be set free, free to be who we truly are.

I contacted Jack and convinced him to come to the Café'. If all you told me about him was true, he would never miss an opportunity to take revenge for himself. Earlier today, I intercepted a call from your solicitor warning you that Jack had been released. I made contact with Shane and eventually he agreed to pass on the message to Jack. If all goes as planned I intend for him to kill me instead of you. I know that he wants to get back at you, his ultimate would be to kill you, but killing someone close to you might be even better for him, but worse for you. Once he has his revenge, he will finally leave you and your loved ones alone.

Ryan, I owe you so much, you rescued me at a time when I thought I was drowning, you gave me a purpose again, restored my pride and faith in humankind. When you bought the Café and offered the ownership to me I thought it was too good to be true. And, all you wanted in return was employment. I know you didn't need the money, you never asked for anything more. Over the years our friendship grew, and I knew that the Lord had given me another son. Ryan, do not feel guilty about any of this. I would like you to go out and live your life, be the man you want to be, involve yourself in other people's lives (I think you know who I am talking about). Now is the time to live and most importantly love." Ryan's voice quivered. He handed the letter to Maisey and wiped away a tear. Maisey read further.

"My dearest Maisey, you are like the daughter I never had. You have shown me what hard work, loyalty and dedication look like. I admire the way you have stood by your son, and how no matter what, you always put him first. I failed miserably as a father to Aaron. Watching you with Billy made me want to be a better father. What I want for you is for you to succeed and make yours and Billy's life more comfortable, so I have made provisions that you will become part owner of the Café and co-run it with Aaron." Maisey, could not believe that Mickey would do that, she could not compute what this all meant, all she knew was Aaron was glaring at her and she felt awkward, but she carried on reading.

"I know you and Aaron got off to a rocky start, but I truly believe you two will sort out your differences and make it work." Aaron shook his head in disbelief, but did not say anything further to interrupt, so Maisey went back to reading the letter again.

"Aaron, I just want to you to know how much I love you, when your Mother died, half of my heart died with her. Instead of focusing on the other half (you), I dwelled too deep on the emptiness that was left behind therefore shutting you out. We had not spoken for so many years, and all of that is my fault. I hardened your heart and now you find it difficult to trust. Please do not be angry with Maisey, she did not ask for this. I ask you to look after each other, and take care of the people who rely on the Café.

Well I better sign off, there is still much to do before tonight.

Love you all with all my heart

Mickey (Dad)"

By this stage Maisey had tears streaming down her face, even Aaron could not fight his emotions.

Ryan got up and put his arm around Maisey, "So that explains all his little trips to "Cork" lately. He wasn't going away, he was going for treatment." stated Maisey.

Ryan nodded and added, "I was wondering why he had suddenly stopped his nightly whiskey with me, and I assumed he wanted to cut down, seen as though he had used alcohol in the past, but clearly he couldn't have it because of his treatment."

All three of them sat in silence, remembering the man who was Mickey.

CHAPTER 29

Victoria felt like a fool, she hardly knew Ryan really, why had she expected anything different. She refused to play the victim, she needed to sort her own life out, and it all started with finding Dermott and making him pay for what he did to her. There was a knock on her door, she looked down she was still sitting on the steps naked. She saw a long coat on the coat stand and quickly pulled it over her body and did up the belt.

She took a quick look in the hall mirror, her hair was a mess and she looked like some sort of flasher but it would have to do for now. The knocking grew louder.

"Alright hold on!" she shouted impatiently. She opened the door, and Liz lunged forward and hugged her.

"Easy there now, what's all this about?" asked Victoria, who was taken by surprise? "For crying out loud! Victoria, two days in row I have had to come here and been so terrified to see what state you were in." Liz punched her playfully on the arm.

Liz looked her up and down "And what do you look like? Why are you wearing that ridiculous coat in the middle of summer?" Victoria hugged her coat closer to her body, her face aflame of shame.

"Never mind that now, why are you here?"

"What do you mean? I went down to that Café today to see crime scene tape all over the bloody place. I ran into Ryan and he told me you had a been through a bad experience, you were fine, but you might still be at home".

"You saw Ryan?"

"Yes, he was at the café, I saw him with one of the waitresses who works there."

Victoria felt a rage inside her, "that bloody bastard, not two minutes out of my bed he is in with someone else."

Liz stared at her, "Oh my giddy aunt! Victoria, did you and Ryan do the nasty last night?" Liz was dancing around her like an excited Yorkshire terrier on acid.

"Calm down, please can I get changed, you put some coffee on and I will tell you everything."

When Victoria came down ten minutes later more appropriately dressed in casual beige cargo trousers and a blue v neck short-sleeved loose blouse, Liz had made coffee and was sitting at the kitchen counter. The coffee smelt heavenly, she grabbed her cup and sat down next to Liz. Liz looked like she was about to explode with excitement.

"Come on spill it, what have you been up to?"

"Do you want the long version or the short version?" teased Victoria.

"I want the version that tells me how you and Ryan ended spending the night together. Oh, and the version that tells me that you were held against your will by a bunch of inner city gangsters."

"You are a very demanding friend, do you know that? You basically summed up the short version anyway. It was Dermott! He somehow was involved in this gang stuff, and when he put two and two together that Ryan knew me, he decided that he would solve two problems with one solution. To get me out of the way and get Ryan to do whatever they had planned for him. But that's what I have to sort out, I have an appointment at the Garda station".

Victoria looked at Liz, "Why don't you look surprised? I thought you would be shocked that Dermott would be involved in kidnapping?"

"That's what I have come to tell you, I heard from Mr Stevenson".

"What did you hear from Mr Stevenson? I didn't realise we were still in the middle of the week. Since I have been off work I have lost days, sorry Liz! Carry on".

"As I was saying, Mr Stevenson called me into his office and he told me Dermott had been arrested. Your name has been cleared. You can come back to work! That's why I was looking for you this morning, I was going to give out to you for not answering your phone, the office has been calling all morning".

She had her job back, she had nothing to worry about and she was on track again, just like before. But why did she feel like it was such a hollow victory.

"Well, aren't you excited, this is what we wanted, you back at work".

"Yes, yes, of course! I guess it's all so much to take in, so much has happened, it's like a dream." Victoria hugged Liz. She thought the news of getting her job back would solve everything, but she knew she was kidding herself.

Ryan had now ruined everything.

"By the way you still have not told me about Mr Sex-On-Legs. So, are you two an item now?" Victoria gave Liz a sharp stare and replied in her coldest voice, "No my dear friend, Ryan and I are certainly not an item, nor will we ever be!"

JANE KEENE

CHAPTER 30

After Ryan had heard what was in Mickey's letter, he knew he had to get Victoria back. He had behaved appallingly and he would be surprised if she ever gave him another chance. After the shooting, the only person he wanted to be near was Victoria.

It gutted him to think that she believed he had used her. He had to hold back the urge to run over to her house right now and convince her of his feelings for her, but the timing was all wrong. He had so much to sort out, and his family was due back from the country house any second now. He needed to reassure and spend some time with them. His actions so many years ago had such a massive impact on all their lives, it was not going to be resolved in one day. He had also asked Aaron if he could be involved in Mickey's funeral arrangements, unfortunately, his love life would have to wait. The Gardaí still had to release Mickey's body for burial, it would be not be long until everything would be finalised.

***

Four days had passed since the shooting, the church was full of people coming to pay their respects, Mickey was well-known and liked in the community. Aaron stood at the entrance of the church, his head slightly bent forward; people came past him and offered their condolences.

He cut a fine figure in his dark suit, tall with well-built shoulders.

Maisey watched him from a distance, she longed to offer him some support, but she knew he would reject all help from her. The way she was feeling at the moment she wouldn't be able to handle Aaron's harsh words.

 Damn!

He was such a frustrating man, how on earth did Mickey think she could run a business alongside someone who despised her so much? Her thoughts were interrupted by Breda poking her in the side, "Do you know I never noticed this before, but Aaron is one good looking man, seems like work is going to be fun after all," she turned and winked at Maisey. "Breda! This is hardly the place or time for any of that kind of talk!"

Maisey didn't know why she felt so angry, besides Breda's usual inappropriateness; it might have been the fact that another woman was thinking the same thoughts as she was. She turned around as the funeral procession was about to start, she did not know how she was going to find the strength to get through this day. But she definitely could not rely on Breda, whose grief had apparently been quickly replaced with another feeling all together.

Ryan delivered a moving eulogy; Maisey could not believe how strong he was for standing up and paying such an emotional tribute to the kindest and most loving person.

Ryan looked at her and smiled, Maisey had been a good friend during this time, they had always had such a strong friendship and it was such a relief to have that now.

He had noticed Victoria who was sitting in the back row with her friend Liz. He felt his heart pounding, she was so close.

After the service, everybody had been invited to the Café; Aaron had argued that it was in bad taste for everybody to gather in the place where Mickey had died. But Maisey and Ryan had argued that Mickey loved the Café, and it was the only place for it. In the end, Aaron reluctantly agreed, after all Ryan and Maisey seemed to have known his father better than he did.

CHAPTER 31

After endless badgering from Liz; Victoria decided to go the Café after the funeral. She didn't know why she was there; she didn't want to see Ryan, but knew it was inevitable that she would run into him, her head spun at the thought. She spotted him across the room, he was standing next to that waitress, and she had noticed the looks they exchanged when Ryan had delivered the eulogy.

She felt a tug of jealousy deep in the pit of her stomach. "Liz this was a bad idea, I don't know why we came, we didn't know Mickey very well, and I just need to get out of here." Victoria made her way towards the exit, but there were so many people crammed inside she found it difficult to move.

Ryan knew she was there, he had been watching her. He could see that she was about to leave so he followed her. Victoria finally made it to the door and opened it, the breeze outside was cool and refreshing. She felt a hand on her shoulder, which gave her a start. She turned around to see Ryan standing in front of her. Her mouth was dry and she found it difficult to speak.

"Hello Victoria, why are you leaving so soon?" She couldn't help but look into his striking blue eyes; he was so irritatingly good looking.

"I came to pay my respects, I have done that and now I am leaving," replied Victoria curtly. She turned to leave, Ryan pulled her back. This only made her angrier. She tried to shrug his hand off her arm.

"Get your hands off me; you have no right, no right at all to even touch me."

"Victoria, please I know you are angry, but I can explain everything. Please give me a chance?" Victoria drew in a deep breath; she rested her hand on her hip. She looked extremely sophisticated in a peplum-styled charcoal grey blazer with matching knee-length pencil skirt.

"I don't want to get into this now Ryan; it's been a long an emotional day".

"Fair enough, then meet me later, at Luigi's down the road, we really need to talk."

Victoria thought for a moment, "Very well then Luigi's at 7, but only for a drink".

"Ryan, Aaron needs you for a second, he is asking for the… Oh! I am sorry." Maisey had come outside to find Ryan, but clearly she had walked in on something going on between Victoria and Ryan. Victoria glared at Ryan who was standing next to Maisey and she stormed off.

CHAPTER 32

It was 7:15pm, and Victoria still had not shown up. Ryan was waiting anxiously at the bar of Luigi's. He decided to order a drink; he needed the extra courage it was supposed to bring. He had no idea why Victoria had suddenly turned and left in a huff. He had just got her to agree to meet him and then she flounced off before he could say anything more to her. He hoped she would get here soon, a lady in a red leather skirt was making eyes at him from the other end of the bar, she had even sent over a drink.

While Ryan was fighting off unwanted admirers, Victoria was still at home in mid debate with Liz.

"You cannot seriously stand him up, Vicky. I know he treated you badly, but he asked for a chance to explain himself."

"Liz, you are not listening to me, one minute he is begging me to meet up with him, and then he is flaunting this other woman in my face".

"I think you are being a bit melodramatic. Yes, we have both seen him with the blonde, but I honestly feel there is nothing going on between them. Don't they work together?"

Victoria drained the last bit of red wine from her glass, maybe she was over dramatizing the situation. After Ryan's betrayal, she was willing to believe that he would be having it off with someone else; it would definitely make it easier to hate him.

"You were obviously thinking of going, you got all dressed up."

"I am not all dressed up!" shouted Victoria defensively. "I live by the saying that "If you look good you feel good." She was wearing a short above-the-knee emerald green wrap dress, it showed Victoria's sensuous curves off in all the right places. The sound of knocking at her front door distracted them from their debate.

"I will get the door, and you pour some more wine," said Victoria on her way to answer the door. It was Ryan and he looked angry.

"For goodness sake woman, you are so difficult!" with that he marched in passed her. She was in shock, but it didn't take long for her to recover, she chased after him. Hearing the commotion Liz came out of the kitchen.

"Liam just called me, we are going for dinner so I better get going." she made her excuses, picked up her purse and left.

Victoria suddenly felt very vulnerable now that she was alone with Ryan. They were still standing in the hallway, Ryan was pacing around. Victoria pointed towards the sitting room and they both went in. He could not sit down, now was his only chance. He walked over to where she was sitting, he knelt down and took her hand and spoke softly.

"It was never my intention to hurt you. Victoria, I think I'm in love with you."

Victoria was taken by surprise; she didn't know how to respond, so she let Ryan carry on. He got up and started walking around the room.

"After Mickey was shot, I wasn't thinking straight. That night I needed to be with you, I needed to be close to you, but when we woke the next day the reality of what had happened hit me. I felt ashamed."

He ran his hand through his hair, "I felt ashamed and guilty that I caused the death of my best friend, and you had been held hostage because of me. It just seemed that whoever was close to me was getting hurt. I panicked and I thought if I left you, you would be safe. But something happened to make me realise I can't run away from what we have".

Victoria absorbed Ryan's words; she still couldn't believe he had said that he loved her. She turned to where he was standing, "So what happened to make you change your mind?"

"I thought Mickey's shooting was my fault, but it turns out he had planned the whole thing, he was terminally ill, and he conspired to save my future by sacrificing his own life."

Victoria felt confused, "But how did you find out Mickey's intentions? Ryan sat down opposite Victoria on a large puffy white sofa.

"He wrote us a letter, me, Aaron his son, and Maisey." At the mention of Maisey's name Victoria felt her stomach contract.

"Mickey explained that he did not want to wait around to die, he wanted to die with purpose. It's all so overwhelming he encouraged me to live my life and be with the person I love.

I also spoke to the investigating officer, he explained about Dermott, and that what happened to you was a welcome coincidence for Dermott. He wanted to scare you, and when they thought you and I were involved, they saw it as an opportunity."

He looked at her as he said this, Victoria had to be sure, she wanted so much to believe him, but there was one issue that they needed to clear up.

"What about Maisey?" she asked tentatively. It was Ryan's turn to be confused.

"What about Maisey?" he retorted wondering what on earth Victoria was talking about.

"It's clear that you two have something between you. Liz saw you two together, and lately she has been everywhere you are. I thought she might mean something more to you." As Victoria said the words out loud she realised that they sounded a bit silly, but she couldn't help feeling like this, she had felt foolish before, she was not going to make that mistake again. Ryan let out a laugh.

"It's not funny, how dare you laugh at me!"

"Victoria, Maisey is like a sister to me, we have worked together for years."

He moved over to sit next her, he took her hand in his.

"I am a little worried though." he said quietly.

"What are you worried about?" replied Victoria.

"You have not said anything in reply to what I said, I am not even sure you feel the same about me".

Victoria moved closer to Ryan, he could see tears in her eyes; she leaned in and kissed him softly on the lips.

"Of course I feel the same way, you dumb eejit! I love you too". Ryan felt his chest swell and happiness flood his system, he lifted Victoria onto his lap and pulled her close to him, and this time their kisses were more intense and held a promise of a night of passion and fulfilment.

CHAPTER 33

Victoria and Ryan were lying entwined in each other's arms, she felt so content and at peace within herself. But she knew in about 10 minutes she would have to get up for work, it was the first time she really did not feel like getting out of bed and going to work. She started to disentangle herself from Ryan.

"Hey, where do you think you are going?"

"I have to go to work, speaking about work, what is going to happen to the Café? Will Aaron reopen it?"

Ryan tried to grab Victoria back into the bed but she dashed out of his reach, he sighed and lay back down.

"Well, Maisey and Aaron now own it together, so I suppose it will reopen soon"

"What! Maisey owns the café? Will you be going back to work to there?" Victoria still felt a little uneasy about Maisey and Ryan's friendship.

"No I am not going back. I don't need to be there anymore."

"But I thought you loved working there? What will you do, how would you support yourself?" The ever so practical side of Victoria was coming through, for someone whose career meant everything to her, it was unfathomable not to have one.

Ryan laughed and rolled onto his stomach, he loved watching her naked body.

"Yes, um, another confession. I, um, I don't really have to work."

Victoria turned from her closet, "What do you mean you don't have to work? Everybody has to work!"

He sat up and pulled the sheets over his legs, "I made a lot of money once-upon-a-time, so I am fiscally very sound, and I never have to work again in my life time". Victoria's mouth dropped.

"Then why were you working in the Café? Surely, you would be on the French Riviera living it up, champagne, girls and all day parties."

Ryan laughed again, he got up and put his arms around her, "Mm, you smell so good", and he nuzzled into her neck and started kissing her lightly. She pushed him away slightly. "You still have not answered my question."

Ryan grabbed a towel and wrapped it around his waist. "After my involvement with Jack and his gang, I went to college and studied hard, formed a business. Lucky for me, it did really well, and somebody came along and bought it for a lot of money. But I always felt that I had to watch my back, I did not want to attract too much attention to me or my family. So, I bought the Café, right about the time I met Mickey. He was getting over the death of his wife, and he needed something to focus on. I made a deal with him that he could have the Café, and I would work there like a normal employee, anonymous just an ordinary guy making coffee. I really enjoyed it; it made me feel part of something again."

"So why don't you want to go back there again?" asked Victoria, she was going to be so late for work, but she would blame it on the traffic.

"That chapter of my life is over".

"How do you know for certain that you are not in danger anymore?" Victoria asked seriously.

Ryan took her hand, "Jack wanted to get me back and the only way he could was by either killing me or someone close to me. When Mickey got in the way of the bullet it was a way of releasing me from that "debt". Even though Jack was killed in the process, no other member of the gang had a score to settle with me, so as far as they are concerned the "debt" has been paid off. So, now I am free now to start over and do something else. Which brings me to my next question. Are you happy in your job?" Victoria laughed out loud.

"Of course I am happy! Why do you think I fought so hard to keep it?" As she heard the words coming out of her mouth, they sounded a bit empty. Since she had returned to work, it was not the same as before, she didn't feel the excitement and same level of contentment she use to feel. Ryan tapped the corner of his mouth in a pondering gesture.

"What would you say about coming to work with me, in our own business?"

"Ryan, I don't know how to make coffee if that's what you thinking!"

"No silly, I am starting up a new IT company, and I am going to need a legal adviser. I cannot think of anyone else but you. We can hold private business meetings, nobody to clock us in each morning." He smiled playfully at her and pulled her back into bed.

CHAPTER 34

The sunlight streamed in through the blinds of Café de Maison, the shop was full of patrons. Maisey stood at the back of the Café and watched people talking, laughing, holding meetings. This is what Mickey meant; the place was magical in how it brings people together. She hugged her arms close to her body; it had been difficult in the beginning and after three months of hard grind to get the Café back open, and of course trying to do all this with Aaron as her business partner.

He had been so challenging to start, but they had eventually worked out a system whereby they did not need to see too much of each other. The main focus was the success of the business and this strategy seemed to be working.

Maisey's thoughts were distracted by the sound of giggling from the office. Nobody was supposed to be back there. She marched down the passage and opened the office door; Breda was sitting on the desk flashing her bare legs at Aaron who did not look too phased by what was going on. Maisey felt her blood boil. Breda was meant to be serving customers not flirting with the boss!

"Breda!" she shouted from the door. Breda jumped up so fast the papers on the desk went flying all over the room.

"Oh, hiya, Maise. We were just discussing this." Breda held up a white envelope with gold printed writing on it. Maisey moved over and took it from Breda's hands, she smiled as she read the contents of the letter, it was an invitation to Ryan and Victoria's wedding. She was so happy that Ryan had found someone to share his life, he really deserved happiness. Ryan and Victoria had invited her and Billy over for dinner a few nights back. Their new house was beautiful, and they both looked so happy. Maisey sighed, maybe it will happen for her, but for now she had other things to focus on. That's when Maisey suddenly remembered why she was there in the first place, she held the door open for Breda and said impatiently "Breda, your customers are waiting!"

Breda pulled a sour face at Maisey, flashed a killer smile at Aaron, and sashayed out the room. Maisey sighed again and shook her head and said to Aaron, "that girl drives me insane. I wish she would focus on her work as much as she does on her social life."

Aaron got up from behind the desk and walked right up to where Maisey was standing. He placed his hand lightly on her arm. She could feel the heat generating from his body, and her body was reacting to it, which irritated her even further.

"I don't know why you are so hard on her; at least she lives her life. Are you feeling a little jealous?" His breathe faintly caressed her neck, and it made her knees go weak.

She swatted his arm away. "Please, why on earth would I be jealous of Breda!"

The whole encounter had her senses reeling; she took one more look at Aaron who was now back behind the desk and stalked out of the room. When she got around the corner, she leant back against the wall; it felt as if her heart was beating out of her chest. If this is what things were going to be like around here, she was in for one

JANE KEENE

interesting year!

ABOUT THE AUTHOR

Jane Keene lives with her husband, two children, their corgi pup and orange Maine coon cat called Pumpkin. She resides in a seaside town in South Africa, making occasionally trips to Ireland and Europe during the summer.

She is a lover of chocolate and reading. Lots and lots of reading. If there is no chocolate, then it's wine, if there is both then she has them together.

She was a teacher for over 15 years and spent a couple years in Europe following her husband around after his business adventures. This is where she started writing and getting inspiration for her books, in the small romantic towns and villages in Ireland, France and Portugal.

You can follow Jane Keene and keep up to date with her latest books at www.janekeene.com.
Facebook: https://www.facebook.com/janekeenebooks
Twitter: https://www.twitter.com/janekeenebooks

***

If you enjoyed this book, then I'd like to ask you for a HUGE favor. **Please, please, please would you be kind enough to leave a review for this book on Amazon?**
Your love (or criticism) would be greatly appreciated.

Thank you for reading!

OTHER BOOKS BY JANE KEENE

Book 2 & 3 in the Café de Maison Series COMING SOON!

Follow for updates: http://bit.ly/jane-keene

RESISTANT HEARTS: A Sweet Contemporary Romance

Read Now on Amazon: http://bit.ly/resistant-hearts

Made in the USA
Coppell, TX
07 September 2021